Zipper
the Kid with ADHD

Written by Caroline Janover

Illustrated by Rick Powell

Woodbine House   1997

✓

Cover and interior illustrations by: Rick Powell

Library of Congress Cataloging in Publication Data

Janover, Caroline.
    Zipper, the kid with ADHD / by Caroline Janover.
        p.   cm.
    Summary: Zach, a fifth-grader who has attention-deficit hyperactivity
disorder, has trouble concentrating and controlling himself until a retired jazz
musician who believes in him gives him the motivation to start trying to do
better.
    ISBN 0-933149-95-6 (pbk.)
    [Attention-deficit hyperactivity disorder—Fiction. 2. Musicians—Fiction. 3.
Schools—Fiction. 4. Family life—Fiction.] I. Title.
PZ7.J2445Zi   1997
[Fic]—dc21   97-40250
                                                                          CIP
                                                                           AC

Manufactured in the United States of America

10 9 8 7 6 5 4 3 2 1

For Jamie
(Our very own kid with ADHD)
with our pride and love

1.

Zach yanked the letter out of his book bag. His teacher had written "To The Parents Of Zachary Winson" on the envelope. Mrs. Ginsberg only wrote letters home if something very good or very bad had happened. As usual, Zach knew the letter talked about something very bad. He hid the envelope under his pillow and jumped down the stairs two at a time for supper.

Zach tapped the dinner plate with his fork.

"Stop tapping," said his little sister. "Can't you ever sit still?" Isabel had brushed her hair before dinner. She sat up straight and put her napkin in her lap. Zach began to tap a quick rhythm on the table with his fork. "If you don't stop tapping," Isabel said slowly, "I'm going to tell Mom you got sent to the principal's office."

"How did you know that?" asked Zach, looking up surprised.

"Because when my class went to the library, I saw you sitting in the 'big trouble chair' waiting for Dr. Jacobs to come out of her office."

Zach stopped tapping. He swung one leg back and forth under his chair and called into the kitchen, "So what's for supper?"

"Meatloaf and mashed potatoes," his mother replied as she carried the salad bowl into the dining room.

"Yuck!" Zach made a face. "I *hate* meatloaf."

"You liked it last week," his mother said, walking back into the kitchen.

"Now I'm sick of it. I want plain hamburgers."

"Too late now," his mother called in an irritated voice. "I spent the last hour making a delicious meal and you tell me you don't like it even before you take one bite?"

"I love meatloaf," said Isabel smiling sweetly.

Zach tapped out a rhythm on his chest with the fingers on both hands. Maybe his mother was in a bad mood because his dad was late for dinner.

"I said sit *still!*" Isabel snarled. "I'm telling Mom you got in trouble. You're the worst fifth grader in the history of the Valley School."

Zach gave his sister a desperate look. "I'll do your math homework," he pleaded.

2

"I don't have any math homework. Besides, I love math. I just have ten stupid spelling sentences to write. The list words for second graders are too easy. I only like bonus words like Tyrannosaurus Rex."

"When is Dad getting home?" Zach called into the kitchen.

His mother carried in two glasses of milk and sank wearily into her chair. "Your father has a school board meeting tonight. He won't be home for supper."

"Zipper got into more trouble today," Isabel said smugly, tasting a bite of meatloaf. She always called her brother by his nickname. Gramps had nicknamed him "Zach the Zipper" because when he was a baby he jumped up and down and up and down in his crib.

"Not again. What did you do this time?"

"It wasn't my fault, Mom."

"You always say that," replied Isabel. "It had to be your fault or Dr. Jacobs wouldn't make you go into her office."

"How was your day, Mom? Did you get any big orders at the flower shop?" Zach squirmed in his chair.

"Stop trying to change the subject, Zipper. What is this I hear about being sent to Dr. Jacob's office?"

Zach punched holes in the meatloaf with his fork. He wished that he was outside playing baseball.

3

"Tuck in your shirt and stop playing with your food," his mother ordered.

"I can't eat this garbage. It looks like brown, baked sponge with gravy on top."

"Then you can go to your room," his mother snapped.

"I'm sorry, Mom."

"I said go to your room."

Zach grabbed the apple from his dessert plate. He ran up the stairs and slammed his bedroom door. He lay on his pillow and took a big bite of apple. He hadn't eaten anything since school got out. The teacher at homework club had shared her bag of pretzels but Zach had only gotten a few. His stomach rumbled as he opened his L.L. Bean backpack. Zach took out his assignment book and flipped through the pages, most of which were empty. He used to be able to remember all his assignments. Now that he was at the end of the fifth grade, it was getting harder to keep all his homework straight. He had finished his math homework in science class. All he had left to do was to begin the research project about the Native Americans of Northern New Jersey. He could put that off. The five-page report wasn't due for another three days.

Zach flopped onto his bed and listened for sounds. He could hear things that other people didn't pay attention to, like chirping birds and bees buzzing up against the classroom window. Once in school Mrs. Ginsberg had asked the class to write down three wishes. Zach's first wish was to have more friends, especially a best friend. His second wish was to be able to fly. He'd be an eagle and soar high above the earth in blue sky. The last wish was to have a million dollars. He would buy his own pitching machine for the back yard and all the Nintendo games ever made. The rest of the money he would invest to help take care of his parents when they got old.

Zach heard a knock on his bedroom door. "The scoutmaster is on the telephone. You can take the call in our room."

Zach twisted the phone cord and paced in circles around his parents' double bed. When he hung up, his mother was waiting in his bedroom. She handed Zach a peanut butter and jelly sandwich on a paper plate.

"I'm sorry," she said, "I shouldn't have yelled at you like that at the dinner table."

"That's okay, Mom. You're a good cook, only I just suddenly hate meatloaf."

"What did the scoutmaster want?" His mother lay down on Zach's black and white checkered bedspread.

"He just reminded me about tomorrow. The troop is meeting in front of the school at 3:05. We're planting flowers at some old age home."

"I'll write a note to excuse you from homework club."

"How come I have to go to that stupid homework club anyway? I'm the only smart kid there. The rest are dorks and dummies and Mantimer's mentals."

"Don't talk that way about students in Mrs. Mantimer's special class." His mother sat up on the bed and looked Zach in the eye. "Everyone knows you are intelligent, Zipper, but you don't work up to your potential. You are *totally* disorganized. You either procrastinate or you finish your work and forget to pass it in. A quiet place to do your homework in school won't do you any harm."

"I'd rather be playing baseball," said Zach.

"When you show us that you are responsible enough to complete all your assignments, you can play baseball." His mother tucked her straight, shiny hair behind her ears. "Until then, it's homework club every day from 3:00 to 4:00."

Zach tapped his foot against the desk. "It's not fair," he muttered. "Mrs. Ginsberg sent you a note, Mom," he said slowly. "It's under the pillow."

Zach watched his mother's expression as she read the letter from his teacher. Her face looked pained, like she'd just been smacked in the shins with a baseball bat.

"We'll discuss this situation when your father gets home," his mother announced in an icy voice. Zach looked out his bedroom window. He wished he was the cardinal flying on strawberry red wings high above the houses toward the moon.

7

2.

Zach woke up feeling hungry. He could hear his dad in the kitchen making breakfast. His mother always left for work before 7 o'clock to buy fresh flowers at the wholesale market. Zach liked eating breakfast with his father. He wasn't mad at him every single minute of the day. His dad was 6' 4" tall. He'd played varsity basketball in college. Zach wished that his father had become an NBA All Star player instead of a house builder.

"I understand Mrs. Ginsberg sent another letter," his father said, reaching for the box of cornflakes. "Your mother is pretty upset."

"It wasn't my fault, Dad," said Zach. "Mrs. Dracula Breath blames me for everything. Even when I'm totally innocent, she yells at me. Just because I accidentally flipped an eraser into Kelly's milk and *whispered* the F word, Mrs. Gambini sends me to the principal."

"You've got to *think*, Zipper! Even if you are innocent, watch your language and never talk back, especially to an adult." His father stood up and lifted the whistling tea kettle off the burner.

"But Dad, Mrs. Gambini is such a big, fat jerk! I had to stand up for my rights." Zach wiggled his feet under the chair as he watched his father pour boiling water into the hot chocolate mix.

"Don't drink this yet," his father warned.

Zach picked up the mug. He took a little sip and winced in pain.

"What did I just tell you about letting that cool down?" his father asked.

Zach pushed away the mug of hot chocolate and quickly slurped a large spoonful of cornflakes in cold milk.

"I suggest you write the lunch aide a note of apology."

"Dad, you've got to be kidding! That lady owes ME an apology."

"Don't argue. Just do what I say."

Zach shook his head and grabbed a pencil. By the time his father had finished his coffee, Zach had finished the note.

9

Wednesday

Dear Mrs. Gambini,
 I'm sorry I said a bad word. I'll never do it again. Please stop yelling at me every day at lunch time.

Sincerely yours,
Zachary Winson

Zach tucked the note in the pocket of his blue jeans. After making a peanut butter, banana, and bacon bit sandwich, he carried his New York Yankee lunchbox into the living room. Isabel was watching a nature program about seals on the VCR. She had already made her lunch and finished her hot chocolate and bowl of cereal.

"Zipper, do me a favor. Run upstairs and get the laundry," his dad yelled from the cellar. "Hurry . . . the bus should be here any minute."

Zach rushed up the stairs and grabbed the dirty clothes out of the hamper and off his bedroom floor. Bending down, he noticed his Boy Scout uniform lying under the bed. Ripping off his New York Yankee T-shirt, he quickly buttoned his rumpled shirt with the merit

10

badges sewed onto the sleeve. Zach wrapped the dirty clothes in a damp towel and raced down the cellar stairs to the washing machine.

"Thanks, Zip," his dad said, pouring liquid detergent on top of the clothes. "You and Isabel had better go wait outside for the bus. Your mother said to give you this note. It's something about not going to homework club today."

Zach snatched the envelope out of his father's hand and raced upstairs to the bathroom. After he brushed his teeth, he glanced into the mirror. He liked his new layered haircut, long on top and shaved around the bottom. It made him look more like a teenager than an eleven-year-old. Zach wished that he'd grow as tall as his father. After baseball, basketball was his second favorite sport.

"Here comes the bus!" Isabel yelled, turning off the VCR. Zach grabbed his backpack and baseball jacket. "Bye, Dad," he called. Leaving the front door wide open, Zach hopped over the wet grass to the school bus waiting at the end of Orchard Lane.

Zach sat down alone in the back of the bus. Isabel always sat in the middle of the bus with her best friend, Liz. The ride to Valley Elementary School took about twenty minutes. Halfway to school, Zach jumped up out of his seat. He ran down the narrow aisle to talk to Henry. Henry was in his Boy Scout troop.

"Sit down, Zipper," yelled the bus driver. "How many times have I told you to stay in your seat?"

Zach sat down quickly next to Henry. "You coming to the old age home this afternoon?" he asked. Henry nodded. Zach noticed that Henry's uniform looked like it had been pressed at the dry cleaners. "Scoutmaster Holmes says we're going to plant some kind of flowers. I'd rather be playing baseball," said Zach.

"Me too," said Henry. "I'm allergic to pollen."

"See you after school," said Zach. Crouching down, he waited to make sure the bus driver wasn't looking in her rearview mirror. On the way back to his seat, Zach noticed that Charlie had a new haircut. Pointing his finger, he blurted out, "Hi dweeb head!"

Zach pulled his backpack onto the seat next to him and reached inside for a snack. With a sinking feeling, he realized that he had left his New York Yankee lunch box sitting on top of the television set.

"Stop the bus!" Zach yelled, running up the aisle toward the driver. "Stop . . . I forgot my lunch!"

"SIT DOWN!" shrieked the bus driver. Her voice was so sharp that all the children on the bus stopped talking. They stared at Zach.

"That kid's an idiot," a sixth grader joked.

Zach felt an angry panic rise like steam inside him. He grabbed the back of Isabel's seat as the bus swerved around a corner.

"I'll give you my sandwich," his sister said suddenly. "Liz and all my friends will share their food." She handed Zach her tomato and cream cheese sandwich and a carton of apple juice. "You better sit down," she whispered, "before the bus driver kills you."

Zach gave his sister a grateful look. Without a word, he slumped back down, alone, on the very last seat in the school bus.

3.

Zach took the tomato out of Isabel's sandwich and ate the cream cheese on white bread for lunch. A kid named Kip from his homeroom and Kip's friend Josh sat down at the lunch table.

"You sure gave it to Gambini yesterday," said Kip, biting into his ham sandwich. "She picks on you worse than anyone."

"Can you believe my dad made me write her a note? He made me say I'm sorry even when it wasn't my fault. Just because the eraser landed in Kelly's milk doesn't mean I threw it there on purpose." Zach tapped the apple juice carton on the lunch table. "So when is our next Little League game?" he asked.

"I think it's yesterday," said Josh.

"He means tomorrow." Kip gave his friend a knowing grin.

"You coming to Scouts today?" asked Zach. "We've got to plant flowers for some creepy old ladies."

"I'm coming but I forgot to wear my uniform," said Josh. "My mom is bringing it up to school on her lunch hour."

"You made an awesome home run in the last game," said Zach. Josh grinned and sat up straight. "I didn't expect one of Mantimer's mentals to be such a good hitter."

The look of pride on Josh's face changed to one of embarrassment. He picked up his bag of chocolate chip cookies and left the table.

"Now what did I do?" asked Zach. "I just gave Josh a compliment and he stomped off like I'd struck him out."

"He hates to be called a Mantimer's mental," said Kip. "Just because Josh is in a special class doesn't mean that he's some kind of weirdo. All he has is dyslexia. He's probably just as smart as you only he can't spell or read too well." Kip wiped up a spill with his napkin and followed his friend Josh outside to play.

Zach wondered why no one invited him to play kickball even though he was one of the fastest runners in the fifth grade. He stood up and pulled a rumpled piece of paper out of his pocket. "Here," he said, hand-

15

ing the note to Mrs. Gambini. "I'm sorry about what I said yesterday." He tapped his foot and tried to force a smile. "I'll never do it again. I promise."

Mrs. Gambini put her fat arm around Zach's shoulder. "Thanks for the apology, Zipper, but you still have lunch detention for the rest of the week. The secretary is waiting for you in the main office."

Zach winced. "I sure wish I could go outside and play kickball," he groaned.

"Remember that the next time you're about to lose your temper. Think before you act. That's what I always tell my grandkids."

Zach nodded his head. "My dad says that too," he said. Zach began to take baby steps all the way to the main office. He hated sitting in the "big trouble chair." Everyone would know he'd gotten in trouble again, especially Isabel, the world's biggest tattletale.

All afternoon Zach felt hungry. On Wednesdays he went to a special Gifted and Talented class with ten other fifth graders. It was hard to brainstorm answers to tangram puzzles when his stomach was growling. When the teacher assigned 35 brain teasers for homework, Zach fell off his chair. Everyone laughed except Mr. Gomez.

At dismissal time, Zach returned to Mrs. Ginsberg's classroom. He searched for his mother's note excusing him from homework club. Remembering that he'd last seen the envelope sitting on the bathroom sink, he begged Mrs. Ginsberg to let him leave without written permission. Because he was wearing his Scout uniform, she said that he could go.

"Don't forget that your Native American report is due on Friday," Mrs. Ginsberg said with a wave. "You don't have any other homework tonight except to read the usual thirty minutes at bedtime."

Zach met the Scout troop on the front steps of the school. Josh got there five minutes late because he was changing into his uniform in the boys' room. Scoutmaster Holmes asked Henry to take attendance. They walked in partners down the hill to town. No one picked Zach as a partner so he walked with Mr. Holmes.

When the Scouts arrived at the Sunset Retirement Home, they saw old people rocking in chairs on a big front porch. Two women with white hair were playing cards. The Director of Sunset House met the boys on the porch steps.

"Welcome, Troop Eleven," she said cheerfully. "My name is Mrs. Brendle. We have a fine group of senior citizens living here at Sunset House. Presently we have twelve residents . . . eight women and four men. They help with household chores such as setting the tables. Our residents range in age from seventy-six to ninety-nine. We'll be celebrating Wilma's one hundredth birthday this August."

"I never met anyone *that* old," Zach interrupted. "I bet she's as wrinkled as a dried prune!" He sucked in his cheeks and crossed his eyes.

The Scouts giggled. Mr. Holmes gave Zach a stern look.

"We really appreciate your help in planting spring flowers," Mrs. Brendle continued. "Many of the stores in town have generously donated the plants and necessary supplies. The tools and flowers are all on the back porch."

Zach started to dash down the driveway. He wanted to be the first to pick out the best tools.

"Not so fast!" called Mr. Holmes. "Please follow directions. You are to work in teams. Each of you was assigned a team and a job at our last Scout meeting."

Zach remembered he had been assigned to work with Henry and dweeb head Charlie. Charlie walked off to get the tools. Handing Zach a rusty spade, Charlie began to dig up dandelions with a shiny, silver trowel. Zach tapped the porch railing with the handle of the spade. He listened to the card-playing ladies brag about their grandsons. He hoped the ladies had made the Scouts some refreshments.

"You sure got rhythm, boy," said a deep voice. "I've been watching you. You tap that spade like Drumming Baby Dodds."

"Really?" said Zach, looking up at a tall black man. Red suspenders stretched over his enormous belly.

"Sure do. I spot talent when I see it, that's for sure. Been playing guitar since I was a kid. Picking Pete Hobson they call me. Ain't no one in South Carolina don't love my music."

"Can I hear you play?" asked Zach.

"You wait right here." The man went through the front door of Sunset House as fast as he could shuffle. Zach could smell homemade brownies. He tapped his fingers on his chest and waited for Picking Pete to return.

4.

Zach wiped the sweat off his neck with the back of his hand. His hair stuck to his forehead with perspiration. The Scouts had weeded the entire front garden by the time Picking Pete returned. He shuffled back onto the porch carrying a guitar case. Zach dropped his spade and hoisted himself over the porch railing.

"Ain't she a beauty!" Pete said as he swung the guitar strap over his shoulder. "Been playing guitar for more than sixty years."

Zach thought the guitar looked like something from the thrift shop. He watched as Pete put a little plastic pick on his thumb. Pete closed his eyes and began to strum. The ladies on the porch stopped playing cards and clapped their hands in time to the music. All the Scouts gathered around Pete. His fingers were flying.

Zach stood absolutely still. He was mesmerized. Never before had he heard such wonderful music.

"Man oh man!" cried Zach. "You sure can play that thing."

Mrs. Brendle walked onto the porch carrying a tray of warm brownies. "Our Pete is quite a legend," she said proudly. "We've got a stack of his records. He's performed with all the blues and jazz greats like Buzzie Holiday and Rambling Spike Cotter. Once he even played guitar in the band with Dookie Voodoo and the Kings."

"You've made records?" asked Zach.

"I made a ton of records." Pete hoisted the leather strap over his head and started to put the guitar back into the case.

"Play more," Zach shouted excitedly.

Mr. Holmes cleared his throat. "Don't forget why we came here," he reminded. "We've got a bunch more flowers to plant and it's already past four o'clock." The scouts took fistfuls of brownies off the tray with their muddy fingers and continued to plant flats of yellow marigolds and pink and red geraniums.

"Sure is colorful!" said a lady leaning on a cane. "I love to garden myself but my knees won't bend like they used to."

Mrs. Brendle stood on the porch holding the empty tray. "We would all like to express our gratitude to Troop Eleven. You boys did an excellent job. Sunset House has never looked more beautiful!"

While Mrs. Brendle was talking, Zach tapped the fingers of both hands on his chest and whispered to Kip, "I'm getting that guy's autograph." He walked over to the rocking chair where Pete was sipping a glass of ice tea.

"Can I have your autograph, Mr. Pete?"

"You got paper and a pen?"

Zach put his hand into the pocket of his Scout uniform and pulled out a squashed brownie. "Nope," he said, tapping his right foot.

"Don't you ever stand still?" Pete asked with a chuckle. "You remind me of my Franklin. He had more energy than all my other boys put together."

"Maybe Franklin had hyperactivity. That's what Mrs. Ginsberg says I've got. She's my teacher. I can't help it. The only time I stay still is when I'm playing Nintendo. It's been that way since I was a baby. Dad says I even jump around in my sleep."

"Sure would be a blessing to have that much energy. I can't hardly make it up the porch steps no more. Can't even stay awake to read the Scriptures."

"I could help you, Mr. Pete. I'm a good reader. If I come back tomorrow would you play your guitar again?"

Pete slowly nodded his head. "What's your name, boy?"

"Zach, but my friends call me Zipper."

"You come on back anytime. I play my guitar every day so long as I don't disturb nobody. I play to Bandit."

"Who's Bandit?"

Pete's deep voice dropped to a whisper. "Bandit is my pet bird. First time I heard her peeping, I thought it was the burglar alarm running out of batteries. That's why I call her Bandit. Poor thing done fall out of the nest. I bought her a cage at the Five and Dime. Don't tell nobody. We ain't suppose to have pets at Sunset House."

"Can I see Bandit? I won't tell anyone. I promise."

Mr. Holmes blew his whistle. "It's time to walk back up to school," he announced.

Zach grabbed Pete's hand. "I'll come back tomorrow after homework club. I can get your autograph and meet the bird."

"I'll be here, if nothing should happen. You're a good boy, Zippy," Pete said with a grin.

Zach stood in line by his partner. He pulled the last sticky brownie out of his pocket and offered it to Mr. Holmes. As they trudged up the hill, Zach saw his mother and Isabel waiting in the green van in front of the school. "Want a ride home?" he called to Josh and Kip.

"We've got our bikes," panted Kip. "See you tomorrow at the game."

Zach climbed into the back seat of the van. "I met a famous black guy. He plays blues guitar. He really likes me!" Isabel rolled her eyes. "Seriously, he says I've got talent. He even said I'm a good...."

"What did you say, Zipper?" His mother turned down the car stereo. "I can't hear you."

"Never mind," Zach muttered.

"No Nintendo until you finish your homework. And don't forget to take the cans and newspapers to the curb. Tomorrow is pick-up day."

Zach stared out the van window. He thought about Pete's bird, electric guitars, the math book he'd forgotten in school, pitching practice, whether he'd sit alone at lunchtime. . . . As usual, thoughts bounced in his brain like a pinball machine.

5.

Every Thursday, Zach's class had a health lesson with the students from Mrs. Mantimer's class. In a quiet, straight line, Josh led his eight classmates into Mrs. Ginsberg's homeroom. Zach beckoned Josh to sit next to him. Mrs. Higgins, the school nurse, always asked people to work in partners.

Mrs. Higgins cleared her throat. "As you know, boys and girls, over the past four weeks, we have discussed the effects of smoking, drinking, and drug abuse. As a culminating project in this health unit, I would like to ask you…"

"What does culnimating mean?" Josh whispered.

"It means ending, you know, final." Zach liked the way Josh mixed up words. It made it more challenging to understand him.

"Excuse me, Zach." Mrs. Higgins stared at the third row. "Is there something you would like to share with the class?"

Zach shook his head and swung his feet under his chair. "No, Mrs. Higgins. I was just mentioning to Josh that alcohol kills brain cells."

"Correct, but I would appreciate not being interrupted." Mrs. Higgins put on her glasses and continued. "With a partner, I would like you to brainstorm the possible detrimental health effects suffered as a result of one type of substance abuse."

"Detrimental means real bad," Zach whispered.

Mrs. Higgins dropped her notes. "What did I just ask you, Zachary?"

"You said not to interrupt. I had to explain something important."

"Kindly hold your explanations until I have finished giving the directions. As I was saying, I would like you to choose a partner and list as many deleterious effects . . ."

Josh put his finger to his lips. "Shhh," he warned.

". . . as possible about drinking, smoking, or drug abuse. You and your partner will then make a poster that incorporates this information."

Zach fumbled in his messy desk for a pencil. "I can spell better than you, so I'll write all the stuff down. You're a better artist, so you draw the pictures. Let's choose drug abuse. Lots of rap musicians use drugs like marijuana. I play rap on the radio all the time."

"Okay," said Josh. He jumped up to get a large yellow poster board from the pile on Mrs. Ginsberg's desk. Josh began to sketch a man holding an electric guitar offering drugs to a little girl. Halfway down the poster board, Zach began to rewrite in his own words information about marijuana. Mrs. Ginsberg said never to copy word for word from a resource book. Zach pressed down so hard, the pencil point snapped. After three trips to the pencil sharpener, he wrote:

1. Marijuana can cause mood swings, drowsiness, and make you throw up and feel real tired.

2. Marijuana can give you dilated pupils and red eyes.

3. Marijuana affects your coordination and makes you act loopy.

4. Marijuana decreases motivation and makes you chill out.

5. Long term use of marijuana affects the
brain, heart, lung, and reproductive system
which hurries aging.

"Marijuana sure is hard to spell," Josh said, staring at the word.

"That's because you have dyslexia," Zach said confidently.

"You pitching this afternoon?" Josh asked as he colored in the little girl's hair. "The Vultures are up against the Somerville Sluggers. I heard one kid on the team is so old, he's growing a mustache."

Zach began to bite his nails. "Coach Ward says I'll either pitch or play shortstop. What position are you playing?"

"Some place in the outfield, I guess."

"You keep working. I've got to resharpen my pencil and get a drink of water. I bet Mrs. Higgins gives us free time if we finish before the bell rings." Zach was glad he'd gotten Josh as a partner. He was one of the best artists in the fifth grade. When Zach got back to his seat, Josh was sketching the rap singer's wild hairdo.

"Zipper, look at this!" he said proudly, holding up the poster. "I made a bubble coming out of the little girl's mouth just like they do in the comics. She's saying 'say no to drugs.'"

Zach looked at the poster. "You *idiot*!" he yelled.

"What's wrong? Don't you like the way I drew the rap guy?"

"It's ruined! The whole poster is *ruined*! All my hard work for nothing." Zach grabbed the poster out of Josh's hand.

"Is everything all right?" Mrs. Higgins hurried to the third row.

"Look what that moron did!" The class got silent and stared at Zach. "That dope wrote 'Say on to drugs!' How stupid can you be?" he shrieked, shaking the poster in front of Mrs. Higgins's face.

"I'm sure Josh didn't write that on purpose," Mrs. Mantimer said calmly from the back of the classroom. "It's a common error to reverse letters in a word, especially short words."

"I can fix it!" Josh cried excitedly. "I always write with an erasable pen." He reached for the poster but Zach held on tight. With a loud ripping sound, the poster tore in half.

"*Now* look what you've done!" Zach moaned. "I never should have picked one of Mantimer's mentals as a partner. Now we've got to start all over."

"You can start over!" Josh said, almost in a whisper. "I'm never going to be your partner, never, ever again."

Mrs. Ginsberg stood up. "Zipper, I'd like to speak to you."

Zach threw the poster on the floor and marched into the hallway, his head down, hands on his hips. "Can you believe what that kid just did?" he sputtered.

"Look at me, Zipper." Mrs. Ginsberg's voice had an urgent tone. She put her hand firmly on Zach's shoulder. "You once told me you want a best friend. Right?"

Zach nodded his head.

"Think about what you just did. You humiliated Josh in front of the entire class. Do you think Josh or anyone else wants to be your friend if you treat people that way?"

"But he made a stupid mistake. It's not my fault he messed up."

"*You* are the person making the mistake, Zipper. If you want friends, you've got to earn their trust."

Zach looked down at his sneakers.

"How else could you have handled this situation?" Mrs. Ginsberg continued. "What could you have said to Josh so you didn't embarrass him in front of the class?"

"Nobody likes me!" Zach cried, choking back tears. "Everyone in this school *hates* me!"

"You are a smart boy, Zipper," Mrs. Ginsberg said in a more gentle tone. "I know you're trying. What do you suppose you're doing that turns kids off?"

Zach was quiet for a minute. "I guess I need to be nicer," he said softly, still staring at his feet. "Sometimes I just blurt stuff out." Zach wiped his nose on his shirt sleeve. "I hurt people's feelings when I don't even mean to."

Mrs. Ginsberg nodded and looked at Zach with understanding eyes. "Try reading body language," she suggested. "Watching kids is a good way to figure out what they're feeling. You'll make a best friend soon. I just know it!"

When the bell rang, Zach followed Mrs. Ginsberg back into the classroom. Mrs. Mantimer's class had lined up. Josh refused to look in Zach's direction. Zach sat down at his desk and closed his stinging eyes. He pretended he was sitting in the final assembly. Dr. Jacobs would take the microphone and ask Zachary Winson to come up on the stage. After being presented "THE MOST VALUABLE PLAYER AWARD" by Coach Ward, Dr. Jacobs would hand Zach another plaque. This one would have his name engraved in gold letters. It would read: "TO ZACHARY WINSON—VOTED THE MOST IMPROVED BEST FRIEND."

6.

After homework club, Zach rode his bike full speed to Sunset House. He wanted to get Pete's autograph and meet his bird before the Little League game at 5 o'clock. Zach's book bag felt heavy on his back. In it he had all the research books for his Native American report. The five-page report, maps on tracing paper, and an illustrated cover were due the next morning.

Picking Pete was sitting on the front porch in a wicker rocking chair when Zach skidded to a stop. Zach threw his bike on the ground and hoisted the heavy book bag off his back.

"How you doing?" he called to Pete.

"Doing real good, thanks be to the Lord." Pete grinned and snapped his red suspenders.

"Can I see the bird?" Zach called, bounding up the porch steps.

A lady with a tight yellow bun looked up from her knitting. "Hello, sonny," the lady said. "What's your name?"

"My name is Zachary Winson but my friends call me Zipper."

"That's nice, dear. By the way, what's your name?"

"I just told you. My name is Zachary."

"That's nice, dear."

"Daisy has memory problems. We're best friends, but I can't say she remembers my name neither," Pete chuckled.

Zach helped pull Pete's large body out of the rocker. Pete's room was on the first floor of Sunset House, next to the dining room. Zach could smell roasting chicken coming from the kitchen. He tapped his chest with his fingers and waited for Pete to waddle down the corridor.

"The men sleep on the first floor," Pete explained. "The women sleep on the second and third floors. Wilma, she's in a wheelchair. She uses the elevator to get to her room." Pete slowly turned the doorknob to his room.

Pete's bedroom was small and cluttered with boxes. His desk was piled with letters and newspaper clippings. On top of his bureau, there was a tall stack of albums next to an old record player. The table next to Pete's bed was crammed with photographs.

"This here is my daughter, Darlene. She's a nurse at Ledgewood Hospital. She sent for me to come live close by. This here is a photo of my five sons. That's Franklin, the boy I was telling you about." Pete picked up a faded photo in a heart-shaped frame. "My wife of fifty-seven years," he said holding the photograph close to his eyes. "Velmetta's been with the good Lord for three years now."

"Franklin looks real nice," Zach said, unsure of how to react. "Your desk is even messier than mine!" Zach picked up a photograph wedged between two stacks of newspapers.

"That there is a picture of me and Baby Dodds. He taps just like you. He's the best drummer in the world."

"You really sure I've got rhythm?" Zach asked.

"Course I'm sure. You got talent in them bones just bursting to be heard."

Zach scratched his head. "Where's the bird?" he asked.

Pete opened a door on the other side of the room. "I keep her in the bathroom," he said, returning with a cage.

Zach put his face up to the bars. "She's pretty cute," he said. "Can she sing?"

"She peeps real good when I feed her. I sneak carrots and apples from the kitchen. You ever seen a bird with such shiny feathers? She eats real good, my Bandit." Pete opened the cage. The bird flew out and perched on Pete's broad shoulder. Pete held out his hand and the bird landed on his finger. Pete pulled a stale bread crust from a tin box and dropped the crumbs into Bandit's tiny beak.

Zach passed Pete the guitar case. "Can Bandit fly free while you play?" he asked.

"Sure thing!" Pete lifted the guitar strap over his shoulder and put the plastic pick on his thumb. When he strummed, it looked like the music transported him into a different world. Zach tapped on the side of Pete's metal bed with a pencil. He hit the light bulb and the guitar case to make different sounds, never missing the jazzy beat.

"Baby Dodds would be proud of you!" Pete's big belly shook when he laughed. "You ever played a paradiddle?"

"What's a paradiddle?" Zach asked excitedly.

Pete used both hands to tap a quick pattern of notes on the back of his guitar case . . . right, left, right, right, left, right, left, left. . . . "That's a paradiddle," he said.

Zach picked up another pencil and tried to tap out the same rhythm. He and Pete continued to make music while Bandit flitted around the room. She landed on top of Pete's head and pecked at his curly, gray hair.

"Bandit wants some attention," Pete said, putting down his guitar. He reached toward the top of his head and cupped the bird gently in his big fist. "My baby Bandit want some attention?" he cooed in a high, sugary voice.

"I'd better go," said Zach. "I've got to write a social studies report that I haven't even started. But first, can I have your autograph?" Zach handed Pete a scrap of paper and one of the pencils.

Pete squinted as he looked at the paper. "I don't write too good," he explained. Slowly, in large, squiggly letters, he wrote....

Zipy,

You got big talent!

Your frend,
Picking Pete Hobson

"Thanks, Pete! This is GREAT!" Zach tucked the paper in his pocket. "Can I come back tomorrow and play more music?"

"I'll be here, if nothing should happen," Pete chuckled.

Zach waved and quickly shut the bedroom door before Bandit could escape. On the way out, he passed the lady knitting on the porch.

"Hello, sonny," she called. "What's your name?"

Jumping down the porch steps, Zach adjusted his backpack and climbed onto his bike. "You can call me Zippy Baby Dodds," he yelled as he peddled full speed in the direction of home.

7.

Zach sat down at the dinner table. He practiced play-ing paradiddles with his knife and fork.

Isabel sipped her milk. "Be quiet!" she snapped.

"Picking Pete showed me how to do this." Zach pounded out a rhythm on the table with extra force.

"Mom," Isabel called into the kitchen, "Zipper is making dents on the dining room table."

Zach's dad carried a large bowl of pasta to the table. His wife followed holding the salad bowl. She took off her apron and sat at the end of the table closest to the kitchen.

"I want to play the drums," Zach announced.

"You what?"

"I want to play the drums, Mom. Pete says I've got rhythm."

"Who's Pete?"

"He's a cool dude I met at the old age home. He's famous. He used to play with Dookie Voodoo and the Kings."

"No kidding!" his father said, twisting spaghetti around his fork. "I'm impressed."

"I *need* a drum set!" Zach sat very still and stared at his father.

"Perhaps we could start by renting a set," his dad suggested, "to make sure you want to stick with the drums." He looked over at his wife. She had stopped chewing.

"Drums make a terrible racket," Mom protested. "The neighbors won't be any too pleased."

"What about me?" piped in Isabel. "I *hate* the sound of drums and my bedroom is right next to Zipper's room."

"I've got it all figured out. I'll put the drums in the cellar. Pete already taught me how to play a paradiddle." Zach picked up his knife and spoon and began to pound again on the table.

"Perhaps if Zipper earns the money to rent a set for a month, we could give it a try," his father suggested. "I've always wanted both you kids to play a musical instrument."

"Are you sure you wouldn't rather play the trumpet or the sax?" Mom asked with a hopeful glance.

"The only instrument I want to play is the drums," Zach said firmly. "*Nothing* can make me change my mind."

"I'll make a deal. If you earn $35.00 and get nothing below a B on your final report card, I'll rent you a set for the summer."

"That's great, Dad, but I need the drum set right now! I can't wait until summer. I'll lose my mind. I think drumming has become an obsession." Zach tapped his chest and looked over at Isabel. He hoped his sister was impressed by such a big word. "As soon as I earn $35.00, can we rent the set? Please, oh PLEEEEEEEASE!"

Zach's Dad glanced at his wife. She gave a quick nod.

"It's a deal," he said.

Zach bounced up and down in his chair. "Thanks guys!" he cried. "After supper I'll start earning money. How much will you pay me to wash the car?"

"And how was your day, Isabel?" Mom asked, trying to change the subject.

42

Isabel swallowed. "I got the worst part in the second grade play," she said glumly. "I have to be the mother. That means that I'm married to that creep, Dexter Smith. Just because we're the tallest in the class, we have to play the parents. I wanted to be the dog."

"You'll do a great job whatever part you play," her mother said reassuringly.

"How was your baseball game?" Dad asked. "I sat next to Coach Ward last night at the school board meet-

ing. He said he was planning to use you as the starting pitcher against the Sluggers."

Zach smacked his forehead. Then he froze.

"What's wrong? Did you bite your tongue?" his mother asked.

"I forgot. I totally forgot the game!" Zach pushed away his half-eaten plate of spaghetti.

"You shouldn't waste food," Isabel said.

His mother shook her head. "You said last night that after homework club you were going to practice fast balls."

"I biked over to Sunset House instead to get Pete's autograph." Zach jumped out of his chair and paced around the table. "Now what am I going to do? The team will kill me. I'm the best pitcher. Without me the Vultures probably got creamed!"

"Speaking of forgetting things, Zipper," his mother said gently, "I talked to your pediatrician again today. I told her that you're still having trouble paying attention and getting your act together in school. Dr. Taibi thinks maybe you should see a neurologist."

"How come I need to see a neurologist?" Zach paced faster and faster around the table.

Dad put down his fork. "Neurologists study the nervous system. They can prescribe medicine to help the brain control behavior."

"There's nothing wrong with my brain! You think I'm some sort of a mental just because I forget things? Is that it?"

Zach's Mom shook her head. "Dr. Taibi says there is a medicine that can help you concentrate and keep in control. She says it works wonders for some hyper-active children."

"You just want to drug me into some sort of a Zombie."

"You're already a Zombie," said Isabel. "I wish I had a puppy instead of a brother."

"Medication may just make your life easier, Zip," Dad said. "You don't lose your cool and forget things on purpose. We know that."

Zach threw himself on his father's lap, wrapping his arms tightly around his neck. "I'm sorry I mess up, Dad," he whispered. "It's easier for other kids to be good than it is for me."

"I'll call the neurologist in the morning," his mother said, tucking her hair behind her ears. "Now sit down and eat your salad."

"I'm not hungry." Zach grabbed his plate of cold spaghetti and carried it into the kitchen. "Besides, I've got tons of homework. I'll wash the car tomorrow night." Dragging his bulging backpack, he climbed the stairs to his bedroom.

Thoughts darted in Zach's brain as fast as a squirrel trapped in the attic. He wished he could write about fighting Indians, not boring New Jersey Indians. Zach pushed away the thick reference book and started to rebuild the moat on his Lego castle. At 9:30, his mother knocked on the bedroom door.

"Time for lights out," she reminded.

"Can't I stay up a little longer?" Zach pleaded. "I haven't finished my social studies report."

"Promise me you won't stay up one minute past 10 o'clock?" Zach's mother pressed her lips on the top of his head. "Sleep well," she said softly.

"Sure, Mom, sure." Zach knew it would be impossible to finish his report in half an hour. After Isabel fell asleep, he'd move all his books into the bathroom. He'd pull down the window shade so his parents couldn't see the light.

Zach tiptoed into the bathroom carrying tracing paper, a ruler, maps, white lined paper, a dictionary, an erasable pen, colored pencils, and magic markers. He propped his pillow at one end of the bathtub and put on earphones to listen to rap music while he worked. It was well past midnight when Zach crawled underneath the covers of his bed. He lay between the cool sheets and dreamed of owning a twenty-four piece drum set with Zildjian cymbals and a cow bell.

8.

Zach stuffed the loose pages of his social studies report into his backpack. He'd planned to organize them in the plastic binder before he went to school, but now there wasn't time. He'd overslept.

"Hurry up!" Isabel shrieked.

Zach's dad leapt up the stairs. "What happened?" he called.

Zach stood in the middle of the room in his Power Rangers pajamas, holding his backpack. "Dad, help me find my shoes. I can't find them anywhere." He quickly dressed and grabbed a banana from the fruit basket.

"The bus is here," Isabel announced. "I made you a sandwich for lunch so you better be nice to me."

"Thanks," Zach said, jamming the sandwich into his backpack. "Dad, did you find my sneakers?" he hollered up the stairs.

"For some strange reason, your shoes were on the bathroom window sill holding down the shade."

Zach grabbed the sneakers out of his father's hand and shoved his foot into the right shoe. He hopped out the front door and jumped onto the school bus. Frank stopped him as he made his way to the back of the bus.

"Where were you yesterday, Zipper? We sure did miss you, man. We got killed by the Sluggers!"

Zach stood in the aisle, unsure what to say.

"SIT DOWN!" yelled the bus driver .

"I better get in my seat," Zach said quickly. As he tied his shoelaces, he tried to decide what to tell the team. He could say that he had developed a high fever and couldn't make the game. Except that if he'd had a high fever, his dad would be keeping him home from school. He could say he was overcome with grief because his goldfish died, but Moby and Dick were still swimming happily in their bowl. He could say that he had an unbelievable amount of homework, but no one on the team would believe that. By the time the bus arrived at the Valley School, Zach had decided to tell the truth.

Zach spotted Josh and Kip locking up their bikes. Instead of going over to the bike rack, Zach hurried to the side door entrance. If he got to class a little early, he could put together his Indian report and no one would hassle him about the game.

"Where were you?" Kip called. "Coach Ward sure was mad you didn't show up. The Sluggers whipped us 11 to 3."

Zach winced. That was the worst defeat all season. "Sorry guys," Zach confessed, "I forgot we had a game."

"You what?" Frankie's black eyes opened wide. "You forgot the game! Give me a break! We were counting on you, man." Frankie kicked the ground in disgust.

"I was checking out the gardens at the old age home and I just forgot."

"You're such a wimp!" Henry chimed in.

"I forgot, honest. I wanted to play but I lost track of the time." Zach made a step toward the side door.

"Get back here," yelled Skidder Malonowski. He was the team captain and the best infielder in the fifth grade. "Face it, you chickened out!" he sneered.

Before Zach could say another word, Josh stepped in front of Skidder. "Lay off," he said. "Zipper forgot. Don't you get it? It was an accident. He wanted to play."

Zach looked at Josh with a startled expression.

"I know what it's like to get teased," Josh said under his breath, "especially when you're innocent.

50

My brother has dumped on me since the moment I got born."

"Thanks, pal," Zach said. He was about to apologize for ripping up the marijuana poster when the bell above the side door blasted three sharp rings. Mr. Maggio opened the door and instructed the students to proceed directly to their classrooms.

Zach hurried toward his homeroom. Mrs. Ginsberg had put a wire basket on the counter by the pencil sharpener for the social studies reports. Zach was the last to turn in his project. He wiped it off as best he could and put it face down in the basket. Mrs. Ginsberg picked up the folder on the top of the pile.

"Whose report?" she asked, holding the soggy cover at arm's length.

Zach swung his legs under his chair. "That's mine."

"I can't accept this report. It's covered with peanut butter."

"My sandwich leaked."

"And I don't see a title page." Mrs. Ginsberg continued trying to unstick the pages.

"I forgot to make a title page, but everything else is there," Zach assured her. "I even cut out pictures of Indians from *National Geographic* for extra credit."

Mrs. Ginsberg shook her head and wiped her long, red fingernails with a tissue. "I'm sorry, Zipper. I'm afraid I'll have to give you an incomplete. You cannot hand in a report in this condition and expect to get full credit."

"But it's my sister's fault. She made the sandwich," Zach protested. "I handed the report in on time, didn't I?"

"The report is on time but it is missing a title page and it is currently unreadable. If you recopy your rough draft and hand it in on Monday, I will only deduct five points from your final grade."

Zach swung his feet even faster. "But Mrs. Ginsberg. . . ."

"There will be no further discussion of this matter." Mrs. Ginsberg picked up the pile of reports and put them in her canvas book bag. "And now class, it is time for the math quiz," she said cheerfully.

Zach felt hungry for the rest of the day. Most of his sandwich had stuck to his Indian report or to the bottom of his backpack. At homework club, he asked the teacher if she had any more pretzels.

"Here," said Josh. He handed Zach three Oreo cookies.

"Thanks, pal," said Zach with a grateful nod. "And thanks again for sticking up for me this morning. I didn't forget the game on purpose."

"I believe you," said Josh, licking the white filling from the center of the Oreo. "My Mom got me a daily planner to write stuff down. Now I hardly forget anything."

"My Mom bought me one of those things, but I never use it," Zach said eyeing Josh's black notebook.

"Me and my teacher decide what I need for each subject and I write it down. See? Look at this." Josh opened the planner to the first page.

Rd. (est. 30 min.)
1. wrt story
2. wrt kersiv
3. 4 paragr.—ink
4. use " " mrks
     (time... 50 min.)

Math (est. 25 min.)
1. p. 93
2. od no. only
3. show wrk
     (time... 16 min.)

"That picture of a baseball bat means we've got a game after school. Badge pictures mean we've got Scouts."

"What's that rat picture mean?" Zach asked.

"That means clean the mouse cage."

"I could draw pictures of Moby and Dick so I wouldn't starve them to death the way I starved poor Jaws."

"Mantimer is teaching us time management. We estimate and then clock exactly how long each assignment takes."

Zach ran his fingers through his hair. "I'm going to find my planner when I get home. I've got to get better organized. My dad says he'll rent me a drum set if I earn $35.00 and get good grades." He popped another Oreo in his mouth, ripped a sheet of paper out of his notebook and began to make a list of money-making projects. It felt good to line up all his jumbled thoughts on paper.

1. Sweep cellar.
2. Clean out storage room for drums.
3. Sweep Miss T's garage.
4. Baby-sit Isabel, the pest.
5. Mow lawn.
6. Weed veg. gd.
7. Wash first fl. windows.
8. Wash car.
9. Write gr. parents.

Zach knew that if he got organized, he could earn $35.00 in no time. He tapped paradiddles on his chest and smiled to himself. He imagined inviting Picking Pete and the bird over to jam in his neatly swept, newly created drum room.

9.

By the time Zach got home from school, he had recopied half the peanut butter-soaked social studies report. Instead of biking over to Citizen's Park to play basketball, he decided to stay at home and finish his Saturday chores. He wanted to be free all weekend to earn money for his drum set.

Zach emptied the trash from his waste basket into Isabel's waste basket. He picked up comic books, Legos, and baseball cards and piled them on his desk. Then he lugged the vacuum cleaner into his bedroom and screwed on the special attachment to clean upholstery. As he vacuumed potato chips off his bedspread, Zach remembered he hadn't fed his fish since Monday. He dropped the running vacuum and sprinkled fish food on top of the water. Moby nibbled hungrily but Dick floated limply in the water. Zach put on the rug attachment and vacuumed the bedroom floor. Under his bed, he spotted the black daily planner. He dusted it off and stuffed the clothes hanging out of his bureau back inside the drawers.

Isabel and her friend Liz peered into Zach's bedroom. "How come you're cleaning your room? It's not Saturday."

"You and Lizard better get out of here or I'll suck up your hair!" Zach lunged at his little sister's head with the nozzle of the vacuum.

"Help!" shrieked Isabel and Liz, running down the hall.

Slamming his bedroom door, Zach turned up the volume on the rap radio station. He sat under his desk with the planner in his lap and designed a time management chart. If he worked both Saturday and Sunday, he figured he could make at least $15.00. Tapping his pencil, Zach heard his stomach rumble with hunger.

On Friday nights, the family went out to The Sicilian Sun Pizza Parlor for dinner. Zach slid into the booth next to his mother. He swung his feet under the table and tapped his chest to the rap tune still echoing in his brain.

"Sit still, Zipper, I've got a headache."

"Did you have a hard day, honey?"

Zach's mother nodded her head. "We're doing a wedding in two weeks and the bride's mother is driving me crazy. First she wants flowers at the end of each pew. Then she changes her mind and she wants flowers only on the family pews. Then she changes her mind again and she doesn't want any pew flowers at all."

"Tell that dumb lady to get lost!" said Zach.

"I kept my cool, but it wasn't easy."

"I'd go ballistic!" Zach stopped swinging his legs. "How *did* you keep your cool?" he asked.

"I used a trick I learned in junior high. My basketball coach got tired of seeing me expelled from games for mouthing off at the ref. She told me to stop and count to ten before I said one word. To this day, I count to ten whenever I get an anger power surge. It's saved me from losing many a good customer."

"Maybe I'll try that," said Zach.

"Try holding your breath for ever and ever," suggested Isabel.

"Let's not say mean things to your brother." His mom gave Isabel a disapproving look. "Zipper, how was your day?"

"Good, except for one bad thing. I think Dick has a disease."

"He's not sick. You just starved him to death," said Isabel.

"Did not!"

"Did so!"

"Quiet! Can't a man have a peaceful dinner?"

Zach knew his dad was mad when he narrowed his eyes and his forehead got all wrinkled. He and Isabel sat frozen still and watched their father pour a glass of red wine. "Sorry, kids," he said. "I guess I'm still upset about the accident."

"Tell us again what happened, Daddy," Isabel said.

"Mike got electrocuted. It's as simple as that. We were up on the job site in Allendale. He got distracted. He just wasn't paying attention. He sawed into a live wire. He died before the ambulance got there."

"I read about the accident in the paper. Didn't he leave a wife and a couple of kids?" Mom asked.

Dad nodded. "He was forty, exactly my age."

Zach hated to see his father looking so upset. "So when can we get the drum set?" he asked, trying to cheer him up.

The waitress walked over to the booth with a little white pad. His dad cleared his throat and ordered a large pepperoni pizza with extra cheese.

"When you've earned $35.00, we'll talk," Dad said.

"I think I can get the money in about two weeks. I spoke to old Miss Tucker after school. She's going to pay me $5.00 to clean out her garage."

"I'll pay you to weed the garden," Mom offered.

"What about me? Don't I get any money?" interrupted Isabel.

"You can help too, Sweetie." Tucking her hair behind her ears, his mother took another sip of wine. She tapped her lips with a napkin. "Zipper, when is your next baseball game?" she asked.

"We play the Willard Wildcats next Thursday. I already have the game written in my daily planner. I'm getting organized . . . real organized."

"Glad to hear it!" His dad gave him a playful punch on the arm. "Get good grades, make a few homers, keep out of trouble . . . that's all we ask for!"

"I'm trying, Dad. I'm really, really trying."

After dinner, Zach climbed into the back seat of the van. It was Isabel's turn to sit in the front seat by the window. His mother leaned close and put her arm around him all the way home. Her body felt warm and smelled of sweet soap. Zach could hardly keep his eyes open. He decided to go straight to bed instead of playing Nintendo or watching TV. Before climbing under the covers, he laid out red shorts, a red shirt, and clean underwear. He didn't want to waste a minute deciding what to wear in the morning.

16.

On Saturday morning, Zach leapt out of bed. He dressed in the clothes he'd laid out on the floor and jumped down the stairs, two at a time, to make his breakfast. Zach emptied the dishwasher as a surprise for his mother. Tapping a tune on the box of Cheerios with the sugar spoon, he slurped a large bite of cereal. It was good to eat breakfast alone. No one told him to sit still, take his elbows off the table, and chew with his mouth closed.

Zach tipped back in the kitchen chair and read over the list of money-making projects in his daily planner. Because he had vacuumed the day before, he crossed off the line that said CLEAN ROOM. The next line in the planner said SWEEP CELLAR. Zach grabbed a broom and ran down the cellar stairs. In the laundry room, he swept around his mother's exercise bike. Dropping the broom, he climbed on the bike. He pretended that he was escaping from kissing girls and peddled as fast as he could. Feeling the perspiration on his back, he hopped off the bike and picked up a *National Geographic* from a pile of magazines next to the clothes dryer. He got back on the bike and read an article about lightning striking a tower in Chicago. It seemed easier to concentrate when his feet were moving. He could remember every detail and build up leg muscles all at the same time.

Zach swept the floor in the storage room and the laundry room. By the time his parents had finished breakfast, he had carried the lawn chairs, skis, Christmas tree stand, suitcases, and boxes full of winter boots out of the storage room and arranged them neatly in the laundry room.

"Mom, Dad . . . Come look!" Zach called up the cellar stairs. "I've made a perfect spot for my drum set."

His parents walked down the cellar stairs carrying coffee mugs. When his mother saw what he had done, she let out a little gasp. "Zipper," she cried, "I'll have to climb over sleds to get to the ironing board!"

"Don't worry, Mom," Zach said confidently, "I'll move some of this junk into the garage. Look, I made the storage space into a drum room." Zach pointed to the wall where the skis had been. "We can put the set right here. I left the exercise bike and two lawn chairs in case my friends want to watch me practice."

"You've done quite a job, Zipper," Dad said, "but I agree with your mother. We'll have to move the sleds and all those boxes to the garage."

"How much will you pay me for cleaning the cellar?" Zach asked.

"I'll pay you by the hour. Keep track in writing of how long you work." His father took a last gulp of coffee. "I've got to go check on the new construction job in Fairlawn."

Instead of asking his father if he could go too, Zach pulled out his daily planner. He crossed off the lines that said SWEEP CELLAR and CLEAN OUT STORAGE ROOM FOR DRUMS and read the next line. The next job listed was SWEEP MISS T'S GARAGE. Zach put on his mother's gardening gloves and headed across the street to tackle Miss Tucker's two-car garage. By the end of the day, he had earned nine dollars. He counted the bills carefully and hid half the money in his fishing tackle box.

When Zach woke up on Sunday morning, he felt a blister on the palm of his hand. After lunch, his mother's friend Nancy asked him to watch her five-year-old. Next to the 2:00 P.M. line on the daily planner, Zach added BABY-SIT FOR MIKE. At least baby-sitting wouldn't make his blister worse. Before supper, Zach scheduled a visit to Sunset House. From 7:00 P.M. to 9:00 P.M., his daily planner was marked HOMEWORK. It would take that long to study for the science test and to re-copy the rest of the Indian report.

Late on Sunday afternoon, Zach glanced at his watch and dropped the garden hose. He left the car dripping with soap suds and peddled fast toward Ledgewood. When he squeaked on the brakes in front of Sunset House, Pete was rocking in a chair on the front porch.

"What's up, Pete?" Zach propped his bike against a tree. He winced as Pete pumped a strong hand shake. He had put a bandage on his blister but it still hurt from so much sweeping. Zach sat down in a rocker next to Daisy. She gave a friendly smile and continued to knit.

"What's your name, sonny?" she asked in a cracked, old lady voice.

"Oh no, not her again!" Zach whispered under his breath. "My name is Sonny," he answered politely.

Pete gave him a wink, rocking slowly.

"Pete, I've been practicing my paradiddles!" Zach tapped his chest with his hands . . . right, left, right, right, left, right, left, left. "Show me a different beat. You can be my teacher!"

Pete grinned. "Used to teach my grandkids. I ain't seen them now for a good long time." With a grunt, he pulled a table close to his rocker. "Pretend this is the high hat drum," he said. "That dish is the crash cymbal." Pete tapped a quick rhythm. "That's the way Baby Dodds played."

Zach mimicked the same beat. "That's cool," he said, trying to tap as fast as Pete. "I cleaned up a place in our basement for my drums. Once I earn $35.00 my dad is going to rent me a set."

"You've got rhythm, Zippy. Ain't no doubt about it."

Zach flew back and forth in the rocking chair. "Did your boy Franklin have friends?" he asked.

"Sure thing," Pete replied.

"Well, I don't," Zach said. "No one likes me. I don't even have a best friend."

"I like you, Zippy. I like you real good."

Unsure what to say, Zach slowed down the rocker. "So how's Bandit?" he asked.

Pete stretched out his red suspenders. "She ain't eating too good," he said with a sigh.

"You think she's sick?" Zach asked. He speeded up the rocker.

"I ain't no bird doctor. It's hard to tell what's wrong."

"You want me to take her to the vet?"

Pete held out his hand. "Sure do appreciate the offer," he said. "Just read me the Scriptures." Pete pointed to a black Bible on the table. "My eyes can't see nothing except what's far away."

Zach opened the Bible to the page with the red string marker. He cleared his throat and began to read in a loud voice, "So Hilkiah the priest, and Ahikam, and Achbor, and Shapham, and Asaiah went to Huldah the prophetess, the wife of Shallum the son of Tikvah, son of Harhas, keeper of the wardrobe. . . ." Zach scanned the page of big words in little print and handed the Bible back to Pete. "I've got to go," he announced. "I'll come back tomorrow after homework club and read more Scriptures. If Bandit still feels sick, me and my dad can drive her to the vet."

"I'll be here, if nothing should happen." Pete waved as Zach climbed onto his bike.

"See you tomorrow, sonny," Daisy called.

Zach peddled hard. He felt a tingle of excitement as he did a dangerous popping wheelie over the curb. It was fun to visit Pete. Pete always seemed happy to see him, unlike a lot of other people.

After supper, Zach flipped through the pages of his daily planner. Next to 4:00 P.M. on Monday, he wrote VISIT PETE. With homework club, baseball games, and trips to Sunset House, it would by hard to earn more money until the weekend. Zach thought about the $18.00 hidden in his tackle box. He estimated that he would have enough money to rent the drum set exactly one week from that minute.

11.

At homework club on Monday, Zach tipped back in his chair and watched Josh pull the books out of his bookbag. He liked the way Josh had color-coded his textbook and workbook covers. All Josh's math books had red covers with purple squiggle letters that said **MATH.** Josh had written numbers in the tens of billions on the workbook cover. Zach didn't think Josh could read numbers that big, but the red and purple covers looked awesome.

"Cool book covers," Zach whispered when the teacher wasn't watching. Josh looked pleased at the compliment. As he pulled out his daily planner, Zach yanked an identical one from his backpack. Opening the planner to the pages for Saturday and Sunday, Zach showed Josh the long list of crossed-out work projects.

"I made more than half the money!" he whispered.

"Way to go!" said Josh. He looked impressed. "I want to play trumpet but my mom won't let me. She says that with sports and my tutor, I won't have time to practice."

Miss Charo walked over to the table. "Remember, boys," she said, "we are here to do homework, not to chat." Zach checked his homework for Monday night. He had decided to take Mrs. Ginsberg's advice and write long-range assignments in red ink. That way he'd get a good report card, for sure. Using a red marker, he planned out how to break his science report into little chunks. Each night he'd do one part of the project. The first night his job was to decide on a topic. Zach needed to talk to his father. He had decided to write a report on electricity. In case he became a builder like his dad, he wanted to know how to avoid electrocution.

After homework club, Zach rode his bike into Ledgewood. On the way to Sunset House, he stopped at The Corner Store to get a treat for Bandit. He had seen bird-seed stuck in suet in the shape of a heart. You could hang it from a tree. Zach took out his wallet and put $2.25 on the counter. The lady wrapped the heart in pink tissue paper. Leaving the store, Zach passed a magazine rack. The title *Modern Drummer Magazine* caught his eye. Zach pulled a copy from the rack and thumbed through the pictures. There were articles on "The Art of Playing the Triple Paradiddle" and "Practical Tips for Rock 'N' Jazz Drummers." Zach gave a quick glance at the woman behind the counter. She was helping a customer. He stuffed the magazine into his bag and hurried out the door.

Just as Zach was unlocking his bike from a parking meter, a man with a mustache came running out of The Corner Store. He looked up and down the sidewalk. The man walked quickly in Zach's direction. "Could I please see the sales slip for that magazine," he panted. Zach froze. He reached into his bag and handed the man the sales slip for the birdseed heart.

The man looked at the slip. "You stole the magazine, right?"

"But I was in a hurry," he sputtered.

The man grabbed Zach by the arm. "I've had enough of you punks stealing from my store," he shouted. "I'm calling the police!"

"Let go!" cried Zach. "You're hurting my arm." The man pulled Zach back into the store. The woman behind the counter was already dialing 911. She gave Zach a disgusted look.

"I can pay for the magazine right now." Zach said nervously. "I've got plenty of money." He reached into his pocket and pulled out his wallet. "See," he said, showing the storeman three crisp one dollar bills. "You don't need to call the police. I can pay the money."

"That makes it even worse!" the storeman shouted, grabbing *Modern Drummer* out of Zach's hand. "If you have the money, why do you steal? I've got kids in college. You punk teenage shoplifters are killing me!"

The police car stopped in front of The Corner Store, lights flashing. An officer jumped out. He ran inside

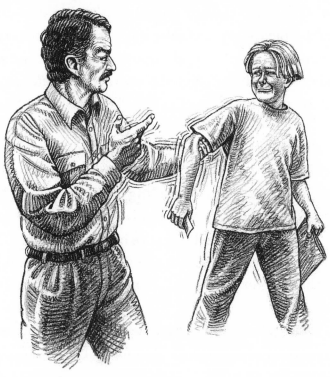

the store. The woman behind the counter pointed to Zach and the owner standing by the candy rack. After a private conversation with the owner in the stationery aisle, the police officer asked Zach to accompany him to the police station.

Zach sat in the back seat of the police car clutching the bag with the birdseed heart. He swung his feet back and forth. He wondered if they would put him in a cell. When they got to the police station, the officer asked his name, address, and telephone number.

"My parents aren't home," Zach said nervously. "They work. Usually my mom is home by now but she's doing a big wedding and today she had to work late. The only people at home are my little sister, Isabel, and the baby-sitter."

"Do you know your parents' work telephone numbers?" the officer asked. Zach nodded. He gave the work phone number for both his mother and father. The officer punched numbers on a fancy telephone with blinking lights and a fax machine attachment. "Your father's line is busy," he reported. Zach watched with a sinking heart as he pressed the telephone number at the flower shop.

"Is this Mrs. Winson?" There was a short pause. "This is Officer O'Connor speaking. Your son, Zachary Winson, has been picked up by the Ledgewood Police for shoplifting. Please come immediately to the Ledgewood Police Station." The police officer hung up the phone. "You can take a seat on that bench." The officer pointed to a wooden bench next to a water fountain.

"You mean I don't get locked up?"

"Not this time, young man. You try a stunt like that again and it will be a different story. Do you understand me?"

"Yes sir," said Zach, pacing up and down in front of the bench.

"I said *sit* on the bench!"

"Yes sir." Zach sat down in the middle of the bench. His backpack made it hard to sit up straight. He swung his legs back and forth, back and forth. He wondered if Pete would still be waiting for him on the front porch. He wondered if his mother would have to pay a big fine to get him released. Zach stood up and took a drink from the fountain. The water tasted stale and warm. He wished his dad's phone number hadn't been busy.

Zach's fingers began to tremble when his mother stormed into the Police Station. Her cheeks were bright red. She looked as mad as attacking hornets. After signing some forms at the police sergeant's desk, she grabbed Zach by the arm. Pointing her finger at the exit sign, she yanked him toward the door.

12.

On the way home from the police station, Zach's mother drove in painful silence. She could not even look at her son. After they had picked up Zach's bike in front of The Corner Store, she steered the green van onto Orchard Lane.

"How could you?" she suddenly yelled.

"Mom, I'm sorry. I did it without thinking."

"Zipper, you do *everything* without thinking! That's just the problem."

"I didn't plan on stealing anything. It just happened. I wanted the magazine and I took it. I'm really sorry. I know it was wrong."

"Over and over you do things without thinking of the consequences. It's affecting all our lives."

Zach twisted the pink ribbon on the birdseed bag.

"Take today, for example," his mother continued. "I had to leave a meeting with the mother of the bride to pick you up at the Police Station. I had to walk out on a major client and leave final decisions and the entire shop in the hands of a part-timer."

"You can drop me off and go right back to the shop, Mom. Maybe that lady is still there."

"I'm too upset by this whole experience," his mother said, pulling the van into the garage. "Do you know how humiliating it is to be called to a police station to pick up your son?"

How do you think I feel?" Zach asked. His heart felt like it had filled with broken glass.

His mother put her hands over her face. "Just go to your room."

"Do you have to tell Dad?"

"Of course I have to tell your father. We're all in this together."

Zach got out of the van, propped his bike against the garage door, and walked into the house.

Sitting on his bed, Zach turned rap music up to high volume. Listening to music and exercise helped to calm his nerves. Zach suddenly hopped off the bed and ran down to the cellar. He hoisted his mother's exercise bike onto his shoulders and carried it up the stairs to his bedroom. Zach sat on the bicycle seat and peddled as fast as he could. By the time his mother called him to come downstairs for supper, he felt more in control.

The smell of garlic filled the kitchen. "Need any help?" Zach asked. His dad was pacing back and forth in front of the refrigerator. Usually he watched the evening news in the living room before supper. Zach could tell by his dad's wrinkled forehead that he was really mad.

"I understand there was a problem this afternoon," he said.

Zach slumped into a kitchen chair. "I made a mistake, Dad."

"A *big* mistake," his mother added, chopping onions.

"I took a magazine without paying." Zach stood up and then sat down again. "I didn't do it on purpose. It was only a cheap magazine."

"Zipper, stealing is serious business."

"I'll never do it again. I promise. Boy Scout's honor."

"I know you mean that, Zipper. You're not a bad kid. It's just that you act so quickly, you don't always use good judgment."

"That's exactly why I want Zipper to see a specialist." Zach's mom blew her nose. "Maybe some type of doctor or therapist could help us."

Tears streamed down his mother's cheeks. Zach didn't know if she was crying because of the onions or because of what he'd done. "I'm sorry, Mom. Sometimes I just feel out of control, like I'm whizzing on my bike but I can't find the brakes."

"Then will you come with me to the neurologist?"

"Does he give shots?" Zach asked.

"No shots, I promise." His mother suddenly took Zach's face in both hands and kissed him on top of the head.

"In the meantime, Zipper, you are grounded until further notice. You are not to leave this house for any reason, except to go to school." His father continued in a stern voice, "There will be no TV or Nintendo for the rest of the week."

"But what about my baseball game on Thursday? The kids will kill me if I miss another game."

"We'll make that decision later in the week," his father said.

"And what about visiting Pete? His bird is sick. He might need me."

"Being grounded means being grounded." His father stood up and paced in his heavy work boots back and forth on the kitchen floor. "I'm really disappointed in you, Zipper," he said.

Zach didn't feel hungry at dinner, even though his mom had made chicken with cheese baked on top. After washing the dishes, he went upstairs and took out his daily planner. He timed each homework assignment and crossed it off the list with a heavy felt-tip marker. Deciding to wait a day to talk to his father about electricity, Zach laid out his clothes for the morning. He put his completed homework and his recorder for music class in his backpack. After reading the required thirty minutes, Zach looked at his watch. He still had close to an hour before "lights out." He took a shower, put on clean pajamas and ran down the stairs into the living room.

"Since I can't watch TV and I have to stay home all next week, can I paint my drum room?" he asked.

Zach's dad looked up from the paper. "I don't know why not," he said. "Just don't make a mess in the cellar."

"Zipper always makes a mess," Isabel mumbled, taking a handful of pins out of the pincushion. She and her mother were sewing her costume for the second grade play. "I bet he drips paint everywhere. Zipper ruins everything."

Zach felt a rush of anger. His heart pounded and he clenched his fist. He wanted to stick his sister with every single pin in the pincushion. Instead, he forced himself to take a deep breath. He counted to ten and marched out of the living room, without saying a word.

13.

On Wednesday afternoon, Zach brought a note home from school. He handed it to his mother. Mrs. Ginsberg had written "To the Parents of Zachary Winson" with perfect penmanship on the envelope.

Zach chewed his nails as his mother read the note.

"Way to go, Zipper!" she cried.

"What's it say? How come she wrote you a note?"

"Mrs. Ginsberg says that you have not missed one homework assignment in over a week! She says that she sees an improvement in your attitude and focus in the classroom."

Zach tapped paradiddles on his chest and beamed. "That's because of my planner," he said proudly.

"Wait until your father sees this note. It will make his day!" Humming a show tune, his mother began to wash the lettuce.

Zach grabbed a sharp knife. "Want me to cut up cucumbers?"

"Not with fingernails like that. Go find the nail file."

"It won't do any good," Zach said, staring at his black and bitten nails.

"Why not?"

"Because it's paint, that's why. It's black paint from my drum room." Zach grabbed the knife and tried to slice the cucumber as fast as the chef at the Japanese Steak House. His mother winced as he narrowly missed chopping off the end of his pinkie. She suggested that he put down the knife and play Nintendo until dinner.

Seconds later, it seemed, Mom was shaking Zach by the shoulders. "I repeat! Supper's ready! I've called you to the table three times!" she said crossly. "How come you can pay so much attention to this silly Nintendo and you can't seem to pay attention to me?"

Zach shrugged and turned off the game. "When I'm *really* interested, I pay attention," he said. "I can block out anything."

After dinner, Zach went upstairs to write an outline for his science report. He had gotten three books about electricity from the school library. After filling ten index cards with notes, Zach decided to take a shower. He was careful not to touch the bathroom light switch with wet fingers.

Zach walked slowly in his pajamas through the living room. Isabel was watching a special about tropical fish. He wished that he could curl up on the couch and watch the program with her. Instead, he walked past the TV and went down the cellar stairs. His drum room was almost complete. He had painted the walls and ceiling black with a white cement floor. He'd placed a metal wastepaper basket, two buckets and a tall trash can upside-down in the middle of the room. The trash can lid hung from a ceiling pipe with fishing line, so he could play it like a giant cymbal. Zach sat on a cardboard box. As he whacked the buckets, he pretended to be a teen rock star. He was number one on the hit chart, adored by millions and millions of fans, not grounded in the basement. Within seconds, Isabel and his parents came running down the cellar stairs.

"What's going on down here? I can't hear my program," Isabel shrieked.

"Listen to this, Dad," Zach said pausing for a moment. "If I use the other end of the paint brushes, I can make a cool swishing sound." Zach smacked his lips, tapped his feet, and gave his parents a demonstration.

"We'll have to buy a cheap carpet to absorb the noise." His mother looked worried. "Are you sure it's not too dark in here, Zipper?"

"No problem," said Zach, tapping the trash can lid. "After I get the money for the drum set, I'm buying a spot light. Right now I had to borrow your plant light from the living room. I even brought the plant down here so it wouldn't die." Zach got up and adjusted the plant light so that the single beam of light shown directly on his face as he sat there in his pajamas.

"This room looks cool!" said Isabel.

"I'm getting posters of famous jazz players to put on the walls. I want to get a giant poster of Picking Pete." Zach tapped the buckets and then whacked the hanging trash can lid. "If I earn all the money by next weekend, can we get the drum set on Monday night? I called the instrument rental place on Route 17. They stay open until 9 o'clock. And can I get ungrounded to play baseball tomorrow? Coach Ward and the team need me."

"That's for sure!" his father said.

"Zipper's passed all his homework in on time," his mother remarked. I think he's earned an afternoon of freedom. I'll try to leave the shop on time and get to the game with Isabel."

"If the plumbers show up on schedule, I'll get back to town in time for a few innings myself. We've hardly had time to watch you play all season." Zach's dad examined the black trim on the doorway. "You've done a very careful painting job, Zipper," he said.

Zach lay under his bed covers. He listened to the sound of the rain on the roof. He hoped the sun would shine by Thursday afternoon. If it kept raining, he'd still be grounded until the weekend. He wondered where birds slept when it was raining. He wondered if Bandit had recovered. He wondered if Coach Ward would allow him to pitch against the Willard Wildcats. It was hard to get to sleep. So many jumbled thoughts churned and spun inside his head. Zach hopped out of bed and lay out his Valley Vultures uniform. He tucked a baseball card of Roger Clemens in his mitt for good luck.

14.

The sun poured through the windows in the school library. Homework club was almost over. Zach offered to help Josh with his spelling list. The teacher said they could work together in the hall if they talked quietly. Josh misspelled half the words, but there wasn't time to keep drilling. It was 4 o'clock and Zach could see kids in green Valley Vulture uniforms gathering on the ball field outside the library window.

Zach and Josh jogged up the hill to the baseball field. Coach Ward assigned the starting line-up and positions on the field. Zach walked over to the pitcher's mound and began to throw balls to loosen up his arm. Already parents were walking along the ball field pushing strollers and carrying lawn chairs. One father began to shoot a video of his son running bases with a fancy camcorder. Zach knew why he was filming his kid sliding into home plate. In the real game, Zach would strike him out for sure.

"Want some bubble gum?" Frankie asked, picking up his mitt.

"Thanks, pal." Zach stuffed a pink slab of gum into his mouth. "What position are you playing?"

Frankie looked annoyed. "I wanted to play short-stop but Coach put me on second." He kicked the ground.

Zach threw a ball in Josh's direction. He ran to the right and caught it in his mitt.

"Nice catch! What position did Ward assign you?"

"He wants me to play the infield and Skidder to play the outfield."

Coach Ward loosened his tie and changed into his sneakers. Zach guessed that he had come to the ball field straight from work. He hoped that his dad would get there in time to see him pitch. His mom and Isabel were already sitting in folding chairs under a shady tree.

"Go Zipper!" his mom yelled as he walked up to the pitcher's mound. The first guy at bat was a tall kid with braces. The catcher flashed a signal to Zach. He threw a fast ball. The kid with braces squinted and swung wildly at the ball. He swung at every pitch, even the one that went on the wrong side of the batter's box.

"Strike!" the umpire shouted for the third time in a row. The first batter threw down his helmet and handed the bat to a chubby kid. He was wearing a Yankee hat instead of a baby blue Willard Wildcat hat. He put on the batting helmet and waited for Zach to throw the first pitch. Hearing a plink as the bat and ball connected, Zach watched with relief as the ball rocketed above the batter's head and landed in the prickle bushes several feet behind the batter's box.

"Foul ball," the umpire shouted.

Zach spit into the grass and threw a second pitch. The chubby kid whacked the ball in the exact same direction.

"I'm not going in those pricker bushes again," called the catcher. Coach Ward threw out a new, slippery ball. Zach lost control of his pitch. The ball zipped over the batter's head. This time the fat kid didn't swing. He froze as the ball whizzed past him.

"One and two!" called the umpire.

"Good eye!" the opposing coach yelled. The chubby kid bent his knees, put his hands together on the bat and looked directly at Zach. Zach threw another pitch. The ball soared into center field. Skidder raced in and caught the pop fly in his mitt.

The third kid up grabbed two bats and gave a few powerful warm-up swings.

"Go Slugger!" came a chant from the opposing team.

Zach glanced over at his mother. It looked like she had her fingers crossed. He threw a fast ball directly over the plate. The confident kid gave a powerful swing. Twice he missed the ball and twice he fouled the ball into the stands. Zach threw another pitch.

"Ball," yelled the umpire. Zach pitched again.

"Strike him out, Zipper!" Zach recognized his father's voice in the crowd. Afraid to take his eyes off the batter, he threw another pitch. There was a loud cracking sound. The ball sailed over the pitcher's mound and landed next to Josh's foot. He scooped it up in his glove and threw the ball to first base. The ball sailed over the first baseman's head as the runner slid safely into second.

Zach blew a pink bubble with his gum and then spit again into the field. The next batter looked like a first grader, he was so small. Zach threw a pitch. The little kid bunted the ball and ran to first base. The slugger on second slid into third.

"Man on first and third with two outs," the umpire called.

The father with the fancy camcorder zoomed in on the batter's box. His son picked up the bat. He looked terrified.

"Strike one!"

Zach pitched again.

"Strike two!"

Zach pitched again. The bat connected with the ball. The kid froze.

"Run! Run!" yelled his father. Holding the camcorder, he trotted along beside his son as he raced toward first base.

"Bases loaded," the umpire yelled into the crowd.

Zach paced back and forth over the pitcher's mound.

"Stay cool, Zip. You're doing a great job." He heard Coach Ward's calming voice over the crowd.

"Kill em dead!" shrieked Frankie's baby-sitter. "You can do it! Strike this guy out.... Strike him out, strike him out!" came a chant from the crowd. Zach could see Isabel jumping up and down.

A kid with untied shoe laces walked up to the batter's box. After a strike and a foul ball, the kid hit the ball. It bounced past the second baseman and rolled toward Josh. Josh picked up the ball and gave a powerful throw to first base. The kid with the untied shoes tagged first base and rushed off toward second. The first baseman dropped the ball again and then threw it to Zach. Zach raced to tag the kid sliding into home plate. He closed his eyes and lunged. Instead of tagging a skinny leg, Zach grabbed his fingers around a thick ankle. He opened his eyes. The man with the camcorder was sprawled on the ground, still filming. His son had made it safely over home plate.

"Two runs for the Willard Wildcats!" yelled the umpire. The crowd went wild. Zach lay on the ground in disbelief. Fury exploded like firecrackers inside him. He jumped up and grabbed the camcorder. "I'll show you a good pitch!" he yelled, marching over to the pitcher's mound. Just as he was about to fling the video camera, Zach stopped. He imagined the consequences. He saw the camcorder hitting the next batter between the eyes, breaking his nose. He pictured Coach Ward dragging him off the field and handing him over to the Ledgewood Police. He saw his dad gasping as the lawyer handed him a $100,000 bill for mental cruelty and a replacement for the shattered camcorder. Instead of throwing the camera, Zach walked back over to the man still lying next to home plate.

91

"You okay?" he asked, extending his hand to help the man off the ground.

"Just a little dusty," the man replied. "You sure can pitch. Hope you'll be on my son's team next year. We could use a good pitcher."

Zach handed the man his camcorder. With a quick wave to his dad, he took another deep breath and jogged back onto the pitcher's mound. Zach threw a curve ball and waited for the umpire to yell, "STRIKE!"

15.

Zach walked triumphantly into the classroom on Friday morning. Kids swarmed around his desk, slapping him on the back.

"Way to go!" shouted Frankie. "You were *awesome* at the game!"

When the principal's voice came over the loud speaker, Zach had his head in his desk. He was hunting for his pencil stub under layers of workbooks and crumpled papers. Dr. Jacobs announced to the entire school that the Valley Vultures had won the baseball game against the Willard Wildcats by a score of 21 to 20. When she said that most of the game had been pitched by Zachary Winson, all the kids in the class began to whistle and stamp their feet. Zach quickly stood up to take a bow. He kept bowing and throwing pretend pitches until Mrs. Ginsberg asked him to please sit down. Borrowing a pencil from Frankie, Zach opened his Wordly Wise Vocabulary Book. He slid his eyes over the definitions. It was hard to keep his mind on word meanings when dreams of pitching at Yankee Stadium kept invading his brain.

On Saturday morning, Zach woke up feeling free. His parents said he was no longer grounded. He sat under his desk and took out his daily planner. Even before he started his weekend chores and money making projects, he wanted to visit Pete. Grabbing the birdseed heart, he ran to the garage to get his skateboard.

. Zach was traveling so fast when he got to Sunset House that he plowed into the garden and crushed two pink geraniums. He picked up his skateboard and leapt over the porch railing.

"What's up?" he called.

Pete snapped his red suspenders and gave a broad grin. "Where you been, Zippy? I ain't seen you all week."

"Sorry about that, Pete. I had tons and tons of homework." Zach paused. "Actually, I got in trouble," he said. "I got grounded."

"Got into trouble many times, myself," Pete chuckled. "Used to get the belt on my backside."

"No kidding! You used to get into trouble too?"

"Sure thing." Pete nodded his head and rocked slowly back and forth in his chair.

Zach sat down in the rocking chair next to Pete and pumped back and forth. "Taking risks is one of my hobbies. I like to live on the edge."

"I know what you mean," Pete said, still nodding his head. "I know just what you mean."

"There's one big problem, though. I'm always getting into trouble. It's like I'm on automatic pilot. I can't remember to remember what I'm suppose to do. I mess up big time!"

Pete leaned over and picked up the Bible. "This book has all the answers," he said.

Afraid of having to read more Scriptures, Zach held up the bag with the birdseed heart. "So how's Bandit?" he asked, tapping his foot. "I brought her a present."

Daisy looked at the bag with the pink tissue paper coming out the top. "Nice of you to bring me a present, sonny," she said.

"But Daisy, this present isn't for you. I brought it for Bandit."

"No one here by that name, is there Pete?"

Pete whispered to Zach, "Let Daisy open the present."

Daisy unwrapped the heart and let out a squeal of delight. Popping the heart into her mouth, she took a tiny bite. Zach could hear the birdseeds crunching in her teeth. He snatched the heart out of Daisy's hand. "Do you think suet and seeds could poison a human?"

Pete chuckled. "I've seen Daisy eat worse!"

"Let's get this treat to Bandit before Daisy eats it up!" Zach pulled Pete out of the rocking chair. He walked slowly along beside him as Pete shuffled toward his room.

"You're such a nice boy," Daisy said. What's your name, sonny?"

"You remembered! My name is Sonny."

Daisy's thin lips curled into a smile. Clicking the knitting needles at a rapid rate, she rocked happily in her chair.

Zach helped Pete sink into the old leather chair. He put Bandit's cage on his lap. Pete sprung open the cage door. Bandit flew out and landed on top of the record player. Zach put the birdseed heart down in front of her. Bandit cocked her head and then she began to peck.

"Don't let Bandit scratch that record!" Pete cried. "I've been listening to Baby Dodds."

Zach moved the birdseed heart to the desk and turned on the record player.

"Baby Dodds is *cool*!" Zach yelled to Pete over the sound of pounding drums. "I want to play just like him."

Pete put the guitar strap over his shoulder. With his eyes shut, he swayed back and forth as he strummed in time to the drum beat.

"Pete, you and I can perform together! We'll play jazz and rap and be-bop and hip-hop and old time blues."

"It takes time, Zippy. It takes years and years to be any good."

"I'm a fast learner and I've got tons of talent. You even said so. If we jam all summer, we'll be ready to perform at the sixth grade dances."

Bandit swooped down and landed on Pete's head. She started to peep. "You want a little treat?" Pete cooed. He reached into his shirt pocket and held a limp carrot stick in the air.

Zach glanced at his watch. "I can't waste any more time here. I've got to make $17.00 by Monday. Dad doesn't think I can do it."

Pete leaned over and put the guitar back in the case. He stroked Bandit's shiny feathers.

"Should I put Bandit back in her cage before I leave?"

Pete shook his head. "Don't want you to waste no more time," he muttered.

"I'll be back when I get my drums," Zach said cheerfully. Giving Bandit a quick pat, he headed for the door.

On the way out of Sunset House, Zach tried to re-plant the crushed geraniums by the front door.

"Thanks for bringing me a present, sonny."

"Sure thing, Daisy!" Zach called. He skated backward down the porch steps. Two old ladies gasped. Zach loved to impress the elderly residents of Sunset House with his daring stunts.

16.

Zach completed his Saturday morning chores. He made his bed, put his laundry in the hamper and emptied the wastebasket. While he vacuumed the carpet, he sprinkled food into Moby's goldfish bowl. Earlier in the week, he'd had to flush Dick down the toilet. Zach wedged the vacuum cleaner back into the closet and took out his daily planner. He read over the list of money-making projects for Saturday and Sunday.

The first job on the list was to reorganize the cabinet under the kitchen sink. Next he arranged his mother's shoe closet according to shoe color and the height of the heel. After that, he watched TV while he built a Lego space station. By lunch time, Zach had washed the inside of the first floor windows and weeded his mother's vegetable garden. In the afternoon, he did odd jobs for Miss Tucker and her neighbor, Mrs. Cooney.

On Sunday morning, Zach counted up his money. He still needed seven more dollars in order to rent the drum set. He was about to mow the lawn when his mother appeared at the kitchen door.

"Telephone," she called.

"For me?" The phone rang constantly for Isabel but no one called Zach except the scoutmaster and Coach Ward.

"Want to come fishing?" Zach recognized Josh's voice. "Me and my brother and Buck have a fishing club. My mom is driving us over to Lake Winacchi. She said you can come too."

Zach paced the kitchen floor, switching the phone from one ear to the other. "Mom, can I go fishing with Josh?" he asked, twisting the phone cord.

"It's up to you, sweetie," his mother replied.

Zach thought for a second. "Sure, I love to fish. I'm coming. When are you leaving?"

Zach had decided where to dig for bait before he hung up the phone. He'd seen juicy worms when he weeded the vegetable garden. Grabbing a plastic cup and a soup spoon, Zach ran outside to dig between the rows of baby squash.

At sunset, Zach returned from the lake. His father had just finished mowing the lawn. His mom was reading the Sunday paper on the patio. Zach showed off his wiggling catfish. "Even though it's not big," he said proudly, "it put up a good fight." He waved the tiny fish in the air. "Mom, want to buy my fish? I'll sell it to you for five dollars."

"No thanks, Zipper. Catfish is not one of my favorites."

"Speaking of money, do you have the $35.00?" Dad asked.

"I just need seven more bucks, Dad. I've got $28.50."

"And how do you expect to get that much money by tomorrow?"

Zach flipped the fish in the air. "I'm not exactly sure," he said. "Maybe you or mom could lend me the rest of the money. I'll pay you back, Scout's honor."

"A deal is a deal."

"But Dad, I've worked so hard," Zach protested. "Look at this!" He held out his blistered right hand. "And my back is *killing* me."

"That may be. But do you have the $35.00?"

"Oh come on Dad, lend me the money, pleeeeeease."

His father shook his head. "A deal is a deal," he said pushing the lawnmower into the garage.

Fresh
Iced Tea
25¢ a cup

Zach threw the catfish on the ground and stomped it with his foot. "I'm not hungry," he yelled. "No one around here ever gives me a break, no matter how hard I try!" Zach marched into the house, slamming the screen door behind him.

The next afternoon after homework club, Zach rode his bike down the hill to Sunset House. He wanted to tell Pete about the delay in renting the drum set. It was one of the first hot and muggy days of spring. As he peddled past the drug store, Zach felt sweat dripping down the back of his neck. An idea popped into his brain. He stopped and counted the money in his wallet. Locking his bike to a shopping cart, he ran inside the supermarket.

Zach stuffed the grocery bag into his backpack. He peddled to the jogging path in the town park and leaned his bike against the public water fountain. On a sheet of notebook paper, he wrote in large letters:

FRESH ICED TEA
25¢ A CUP

Zach took a bag of ice and a stack of paper cups out of the grocery bag. He dropped three ice cubes and a scoop of instant ice tea mix into each cup. Then he filled the cups with water from the drinking fountain.

"Ice cold, ice tea!" Zach yelled in a loud voice. Three teenagers on in-line skates stopped to buy drinks. A man walking his dog drank one cup and then asked for another. A lady jogged by, bought a cup of ice tea, and then poured it on top of her head. People bought drinks almost as fast as Zach could fill the cups. A line of thirsty Girl Scouts waited patiently for a cool drink. They'd been at the park since school got out to pick up trash from the parking lot and pathways.

Zach rode his bike home just in time for supper. "I did it!" he cried, bursting open the screen door.

"Where have you been, Zipper? I was getting worried."

"Mom, look. I've got the money!" Zach held up four paper cups full of coins.

"But how did. . . .?"

"Where there's a will, there's a way!" Zach said triumphantly. He handed his mother the half-empty can of instant ice tea mix and dashed up the stairs to get the money hidden in his tackle box. Zach piled $39.50 in front of his father's dinner plate.

"I made a little extra to buy a cowbell," Zach said.

"Your father will be mighty impressed. He never thought you'd earn all that money so quickly!"

Isabel skipped into the dining room. She took one look at the cash piled on the table and let out a gasp. "I knew it! Now Zipper is robbing banks! Pretty soon he'll get put in jail."

"Don't talk about your brother like that! He earned every penny."

Isabel slumped into her seat at the dinner table. "Great," she groaned. "Now I'll have to listen to pounding drums day and night."

"You'll love it!" Zach replied with a grin.

17.

Zach put a phone book on top of the cardboard box to make his drum stool taller. He sat up straight, the five-piece drum set with high-hat Zildjian cymbals and the cowbell carefully arranged in front of him. It had taken Zach and his father more than an hour to put the set together. When Zach tapped his foot, a pedal hit the big bass drum with a thud. He practiced new rhythms by hitting the snare drum and crash cymbal with the wooden drum sticks. They had also rented a pair of wire brushes. Zach liked the wooden sticks better. They made more noise.

Unless there was a Little League game or a Boy Scout meeting, Zach came directly home after school. He tried to force himself to focus every minute in home-work club. If he didn't whisper to Josh, doodle, day-dream, or write rap tunes, he could complete all his homework. When Zach got home, he ran directly to the cellar. He'd grab his drum sticks and invent new rhythms until supper time.

"You sound better than you did a month ago," his mother said one night at dinner.

"If you ask me, Zipper sounds worse," Isabel said. "The more he practices, the louder he gets."

"Pete is lending me more Baby Dodds records. He showed me a double paradiddle today." Zach tapped his glass with his fork.

"Maybe one day you'll turn into a Ringo Starr," his dad replied. "He's earned more money playing drums than I'll see in a lifetime."

"I aim to tour with a band like Phish or Zestfinger. Picking Pete might be too old to tour, even though he's already famous."

"Speaking of Picking Pete," his mother said, "the Fourth of July Float Committee met last night at Kip's house. His name came up as a possible performer."

"Pete on guitar and me on drums!" Zach shouted. "We can sit on a flatbed truck surrounded by American flags."

Isabel gulped her milk. "Liz and I could hold the Valley School banner!"

"It's just an idea, kids. Nothing definite. The entire committee has to vote on the decision."

After supper, Zach put his Yankee baseball cap on backward and jumped down the cellar stairs to his drum room. He hung up new posters of Miles Davis, The Beatles, and The Raving Rap Be-Bop Boys. He focused the beam of the plant light on the bass drum and began to play along to Phish's latest CD.

At lunch time the next day, the Phish music still echoed in his brain. Zach ate quickly so he could get outside to play. Mrs. Gambini stopped him at the cafeteria door. She handed him a smelly, yellow sponge and said it was his turn to wipe the tables. By the time Zach finished cleaning the tables, the playground was crowded with kids playing kickball or shooting hoops on the blacktop. Zach grabbed a ball out of a second grader's hand and cut in front of the basket.

"Wait your turn, kid," a voice yelled. Zach bounced the basketball and took aim. A tall girl wearing high top sneakers held up her hand to block the shot. "I said, wait your turn!"

"But I just got here. Gambini made me wipe tables." Zach pushed the girl's arm away and threw the ball into the basket.

"See all those kids?" the girl asked, grabbing the ball. "All those kids are waiting in line to shoot. You can't just butt in!"

"Don't you understand? I just got out here! If I don't shoot now, recess will be over before I get a chance to play." Zach tried to snatch the ball out of the girl's hands. She held tight.

"Oh no, you don't," she yelled. Zach and the tall girl tugged wildly at the ball. Kids crowded around to watch the action. Just as Mrs. Gambini elbowed her way into the cheering crowd, the girl hurled the ball at Zach. "Here! Take it."

The ball smashed Zach in the face. Blood gushed from his nose. Such pain throbbed between Zach's eyes, he thought he was going to faint.

"Call an ambulance," he moaned, licking blood off his lips.

"Go get Mrs. Higgins," Mrs. Gambini yelled to a fifth grader. "Tell her there is a lot of blood."

Zach sat down on the ground. Josh knelt down beside him. "You okay, man?" he asked.

Mrs. Higgins arrived wearing rubber gloves and carrying a towel. She walked with Zach back to her office. Josh asked if he could come too but Mrs. Higgins said that wouldn't be necessary. The nurse gently wiped the blood off Zach's face with damp cotton balls. "I'll call your mother at work. She may want to take you to the doctor for an x-ray. Hold this ice pack up to your nose."

The nurse left to use the phone in the main office. A kid wearing a colorful, short-sleeved Hawaiian shirt walked in the door.

"What happened?" he asked, staring at Zach's bloody T-shirt.

"I've got a broken nose. It kills! Are you injured too?"

The kid shook his head. "I'm fine. I just came to get my medicine."

"If you're fine, how come you need medicine?" Zach asked.

"It's my brain pill. It calms me down so I can think."

"Does it make you smarter?"

"No way. It just helps me pay attention. Now I can sit still even in boring classes. Before I took my brain pill, I bounced off the walls. Everyone said so, even my girlfriend."

"You've got a girlfriend?" Zach asked.

"Girls go crazy over me. I think it's my charisma."

Mrs. Higgins hurried back into the office. "Your mother is on her way," she said to Zach. She handed the boy in the Hawaiian shirt a little pill and a paper cup full of water.

"Enjoy the afternoon, Tucker," she said as he swallowed the pill.

"I usually do!" he replied cheerfully. "Hope your nose feels better." He gave Zach a quick high five and hurried back to class.

"Such a nice boy!" Mrs. Higgins exclaimed.

Zach pressed the ice pack to his throbbing nose. He wished he could take a pill to make the pain in his nose and the noise in his brain go away.

18.

Zach and Josh sat at the kitchen table eating ice cream sandwiches. Isabel and Liz decided to eat their ice cream sandwiches on the swing set in the back yard.

"Your eye looks gross," Josh said, wiping his mouth with the back of his hand.

"My nose got smashed more than a week ago and it's still swollen. Now my black eye is turning green!"

"Did it hurt when you went to the doctor?" Josh asked.

"It killed! He twisted and squeezed my nose and took an x-ray. Then he said it wasn't broken," Zach replied.

"My doctor is real gentle." Josh licked ice cream off his finger.

"When I went to the neurologist, that doctor didn't hurt at all. He measured my head and told me to close my eyes and touch my nose with my eyes closed. My nose was so swollen I found it instantly!" Zach closed his eyes and showed Josh how he had to touch his nose with his finger.

"I can do that," said Josh. He put a sticky smudge of chocolate ice cream on the end of his nose.

"The neurologist says I might have ADDH or ADHD, something like that. He might give me pills to help me pay attention." Zach wiggled his feet. "He says the messenger service in my brain could be screwed up. It's like fixing the brakes on a racing car. He said Mrs. Ginsberg was really smart to pinpoint my problem. Now she and my parents have to fill out this long questionnaire."

"My parents had to fill out forms about my dyslexia. What kind of questions did they ask?"

"They wanted to know stuff like do I fidget and blurt out answers and have trouble waiting my turn. They also wanted to know how long the problem has been going on. Mom said I've had ADHD since before I got born. It's in your brain. You can't catch it."

"You can't catch dyslexia either," Josh said. "That's what's in my brain. You can be really, really smart and still have dyslexia."

"You can be really, really smart and have ADHD. Just look at me!"

Isabel opened the screen door. "How come you've got chocolate on your noses?" she asked.

"Want to hear my drums?" Zach carefully wiped the chocolate off the end of his tender nose.

Isabel, Liz, and Josh followed Zach as he raced down the cellar stairs. He turned on the plant light and picked up his drumsticks. With his right foot pumping the bass drum pedal, he crashed out a rhythm on the snare drum. He tapped the cowbell with the tip of his stick. Zach closed his eyes and pretended that he was performing in front of every kid at Valley School. They'd be cheering and stomping their feet, even the kindergartners.

"Cool!" Josh said.

Zach turned on the record of Picking Pete playing guitar with Dookie Voodoo and the Kings. Isabel tapped her foot in time to the rhythm as Zach played along with the band. "That's my favorite record," Isabel said. "Zach also plays to The Beatles and Phish, but I like Dookie the best." Isabel flipped her ponytail behind her back. "Zach and I might be in the Fourth of July parade. We might be on a big truck with Picking Pete. I'd get to hold the Valley School banner and wave to the crowds."

"I'm bored," said Liz. "Let's go over to my house."

Zach tapped the crash cymbal and flipped the drumsticks in the air. "Lizard doesn't appreciate good music," he said.

After the girls had left the cellar, Josh got off the exercise bike and asked to see Zach's signed Dave Winfield baseball card. Up in his room, Zach took albums of baseball cards out from under the pile of dirty clothes on his closet floor. The boys sat on Zach's bed and thumbed through pages and pages of baseball cards.

"You pitching on Saturday against the Tigers?" Josh asked.

Zach hopped off the bed and whirled his arm in circles, pretending to throw balls over the plate.

"Without you, we'd never have made the finals. You're the best pitcher in the league. Everyone says so, even Skidder."

Zach grinned. He sat down and swung his feet back and forth under the bed.

"The Tigers have a girl pitcher."

"No way!"

"She's awesome. She's taller than Skidder. I know because she goes to my church. Her name is Bootsie MacGregor."

Zach picked up another album of baseball cards and handed it to Josh. "My grandfather is coming to the game on Saturday. It's my Dad's birthday and he wants to see me pitch. Gramps used to watch the Dodgers play at Ebbets field. Once he even met Jackie

Robinson face to face. After the game, we're having a cookout." Zach paused. "Maybe you can come too!"

"I'll ask my mom," Josh said. "What time is it?"

Zach held out his wrist and showed him his watch.

"Just tell me the time. I only read digital watches."

"It's 4:55. That means it's almost 5 o'clock. You want to throw some balls in the backyard before you go home?"

"I didn't finish my math in homework club. I've got to go." Josh stood up and straightened Zach's rumpled bedspread.

On the way out, Josh called into the kitchen, "Thanks for the ice cream sandwich, Mrs. Wilson."

Zach closed the screen door. "Can Josh come to Dad's cookout?" he asked. "I want Gramps to meet my best friend."

His mother smiled and picked up a scrubbed potato. "Even though Josh can't seem to remember our last name, he's welcome to join us."

Zach skipped down the cellar stairs. He wanted to practice the drums until supper. Zach had decided to compose a drum rap tune in honor of his father. He would play it for him on June 9, his father's forty-first birthday.

19.

On June 9, the chirping birds woke Zach at dawn. Even though it was 5:28 in the morning, he could not get back to sleep. His eyes were closed but racing thoughts bombarded his brain. Zach got up and took a shower. He wanted the steam to loosen his pitching arm. He buttoned his Valley Vultures uniform and slid down the banister. After he ate cereal and vacuumed his bedroom, there was just enough time to skateboard over to Sunset House. Coach Ward wanted the team to report to the baseball field by 9:30 to warm up for the 10 o'clock game. They had played the first-place Travell Tigers once before. The Vultures had lost the game by a score of 11 to 7. Even as the underdogs, Coach Ward felt confident they could pull off a victory. He said it would take teamwork, luck, and superior coaching.

Zach got to Sunset House so early that Pete and Daisy were not yet outside. He put the skateboard on Pete's rocker and jogged down the dark hallway. Zach tapped on Pete's bedroom door.

"Door's open," Pete called.

Zach flopped onto Pete's unmade bed. "Want to come to my house for a cookout today?" he panted. "My Dad wants you to come. It's his birthday." Zach stopped to catch his breath. "My grandfather is taking the bus from the city to watch me play baseball and help my dad with the barbecue. Gramps has heard of you! He wants you to autograph his Dookie Voodoo and the Kings album cover. Dad can pick you up after the game. So can you come?"

"I don't know, Zippy," he said. "Been feeling as tired as a coon dog in the summer time. My Darlene is coming over to take a look at me."

"Couldn't your daughter come another time? You could bring your guitar and listen to me play drums. You won't need to climb down the cellar stairs. Mom says you can hear the drums in every room of the house."

Pete shook his head. "I'm waiting for Darlene to bring me medicine. I'll have to come over some other day."

Zach turned his baseball cap around backward. "You seem okay to me, Pete. You look a lot better than you did last week."

Bandit flew from her perch on top of the bureau and landed on Pete's shoulder. "You positive you can't come?" Zach asked.

Pete shook his head. "I may not even make it to the front porch today," he said.

Zach opened the door to leave. "I'll come back later and check up on you. Right now I'm pitching the. . . ." There was a sudden flutter of wings. Bandit hopped off Pete's shoulder and flew above Zach's head out the open door. Zach gasped and followed her down the corridor.

"She flew into the kitchen!" Zach ran back to Pete's room and pulled him out of his sagging, leather chair.

Pete shuffled down the hall, holding up his trousers. He had no time to put on his red suspenders. "We've got to catch her before cook sees her," he muttered.

Zach pointed. "She's up on those ceiling pipes."

"Here, sweetie," Pete cooed. "Come here to daddy."

Bandit flew from one pipe to another. "I'll climb up and catch her," Zach cried. He jumped up on the counter. Standing on his tiptoes, he snatched at the bird. Bandit hopped to another pipe just out of reach.

Pete closed the kitchen door. "Mrs. Brendle hears us we'll be in big trouble," he warned. "Ain't no pets allowed in Sunset House. They'll put me on the streets if they see I got me a bird."

"Don't you worry, Pete. I'll catch her." Zach jumped off the counter. "Quick, find me a sieve."

The kitchen door opened a crack. "What's all this clatter?" Daisy stood in her bathrobe and bedroom slippers, holding her bag of knitting and a toothbrush.

"Close the door!" Pete cried. "Bandit's done gone and escaped."

Daisy shut the door and looked up at the ceiling pipes. "What's your name, sonny?" she asked, startled, as Zach stepped out of the cleaning closet holding a broom handle.

"Did you find the sieve?" Zach asked, ignoring Daisy's question.

"Cook uses this for spaghetti," Pete said, handing him a large sieve.

"Now I need masking tape or string," Zach said.

Daisy reached into her knitting bag and pulled out a ball of yellow yarn. "Will this do?" she asked.

"Perfect!" said Zach. He grabbed the yarn out of Daisy's hand and tied the sieve tightly to the end of the broom handle.

"You made a butterfly net!" Daisy cried excitedly.

Zach climbed back onto the kitchen counter. He swooped the sieve back and fourth in front of Bandit. She dodged each pass and flew to the top of the refrigerator.

Pete took a giant jar out of the food cabinet. With his finger, he spread a glob of peanut butter on top of a cracker. Then he sprinkled poppy seeds on top of the peanut butter. "Put this in the sieve and leave it still," he said.

Slowly Zach lifted the broom handle toward the ceiling. Bandit flew off the refrigerator and perched on the side of the sieve. She began to peck hungrily at the seeds stuck into the peanut butter.

"Get the birdcage," Pete whispered. Daisy dropped her knitting bag and hurried away. She returned carrying an alarm clock. "The birdcage!" Pete repeated gruffly.

Daisy scurried back down the hall mumbling "birdcage, birdcage" under her breath.

Zach stood perfectly still, afraid Bandit would fly back to the ceiling pipes with any sudden motion. Very slowly, he lowered the sieve. Pete put a dab of peanut butter on the end of his finger. He held his hand still in front of Bandit.

"Ouch!" Bandit pecked at Pete's finger. He gently cupped her in his huge fist and placed her gently on the counter. Zach clapped the sieve over her and waited for Daisy. She returned swinging the birdcage in one hand and her suitcase in the other. Pete quickly locked Bandit in the cage and licked the peanut butter off his finger.

"The coast is clear!" Zach peered into the hallway. "Follow me," he whispered. Halfway down the corridor, Mrs. Brendle suddenly appeared from the front office. Zach grabbed Daisy's hand. He pulled her close beside him to hide Pete, who was shuffling along behind them, holding up his pants and carrying Bandit's cage.

"There's been a break-in!" Mrs. Brendle sputtered. "Some of the residents reported loud noises coming from the kitchen. Cook is at the market. I've called the police."

"Good thinking!" said Zach. "I'll make sure that Pete and Daisy are safe." He pushed Daisy along the corridor.

Daisy stopped and turned to Mrs. Brendle. "He's so clever," she said. "This nice boy....What's your name again, sonny?"

"Walk quickly, Daisy. There's a robber loose in the kitchen."

"My lands!" Daisy exclaimed. "We haven't had this much excitement around here since Wilma found her false teeth in the freezer!"

Pete started to hum a spiritual in a low, deep voice. Bandit was peeping in her cage. Zach joined the singing and bellowed out a verse of "Go Down Moses." "This is the time you need the protection of the Lord," he explained to Mrs. Brendle as they continued their slow shuffle down the hall.

Back in Pete's bedroom, Zach looked at his watch. It said 10:19. "I'm out of here!" he cried. With a sinking heart, he dashed toward the front door. Zach jumped on his skateboard and raced through red lights to the baseball field.

20.

Zach picked up his skateboard and ran up the grassy hill to the baseball field. He saw a woman pacing back and forth under the trees, away from the crowd.

"How could you?" His mother marched toward him, arms folded over her chest. "How could you embarrass us like this? Your grandfather takes the bus all the way from New York City to watch you play baseball and you aren't even at the field!"

"I'm sorry, Mom. An emergency came up I had to deal with."

Zach and his mother jogged toward the playing field. One foot tagging third base, Josh spotted them coming. He shrieked to the team in an excited voice, "He made it! Zipper is here!"

Zach could tell by his Dad's squinting eyes that he was upset. "Where on earth have you been?" he demanded. "You should have been on the field over an hour ago."

"Zipper forgets to come to the close games," yelled a voice from the outfield.

"I DIDN'T forget!" Zach protested. "I had to catch Bandit."

"Oh great! Now you're going to make up some wild story about catching robbers." His mother looked even angrier. "You have a vivid imagination when it comes to making up excuses."

"Give the kid a break," his father interrupted.

"I went to Sunset House to invite Pete to our cookout." Zach's voice cracked. "But his bird escaped. Pete was really upset. You can get kicked out of the old age home if you try to hide a pet."

"Did you catch it?" his father asked.

"I tied a sieve to a broom handle and trapped it."

"Clever thinking! Is Pete coming over for lunch?"

"Pete wants to come but he doesn't feel well." Zach picked up his mitt and punched his fist into the glove.

"We missed you, Zipper." Coach Ward took off his Vulture baseball cap and scratched his balding head. "Tigers are in the lead. You ready to pitch the next inning?"

"Sure!" said Zach, tapping paradiddles on his chest. "I'll go throw a few balls with my Dad to loosen up my arm."

"First you're up at bat." Coach Ward walked over to talk to the umpire.

"Go Zipper!" Gramps yelled from the sidelines.

Josh, one foot still touching third base, stood poised to run. "Bring me home," he called. "I'm homesick!" The bases were loaded. Zach put his feet together, bent his knees and gripped the bat with both hands. The girl pitcher made him nervous. She had wild, lobster red hair and a powerful fast ball.

"Strike," yelled the umpire.

Zach tapped the batter's mound and raised his bat.

"Good eye!" called his Dad. "Eye on the ball."

Zach swung at the second pitch. The ball popped into the air and landed behind the batter's cage next to Isabel's foot. "He's trying to kill me!" his sister cried.

"Strike him out, Bootsie!" roared the Tigers.

"Zipper, you can do it!" Zach could hear his grandfather's excited voice calling from the row of lawn chairs. He took a deep breath and pounded the plate. Focusing all his powers of concentration on the ball, he gave a mighty swing. The ball rocketed deep into left field. Zach ran. He ran with electric energy. Tagging all the bases with his foot, he dove for home plate. Cheers and hoots erupted from the crowd.

"Safe!" yelled the Umpire. "HOME RUN!" The crowd went wild. His teammates mobbed him, slamming him on the back. Zach stood up and staggered

toward the dugout. He looked into the crowd. His Dad and Gramps were hugging each other. His Mom was jumping up and down. Even Isabel looked excited.

"He's my brother!" she shouted to Coach Ward.

Skidder handed Zach a paper cup of Gatorade. "Championship, here we come!" he shouted to the crowd. At the end of the game, the team gathered around Coach Ward in the middle of the field. "Two, four, six, eight . . . Who do we appreciate . . . Travell Tigers!" they chanted victoriously. Zach felt like a hero. Suddenly, the whole world wanted to be his friend.

On the way home from the game, Zach got to sit in the front seat next to Gramps. Isabel and his mother sat in the back seat with the skateboard and lawn chairs.

"You're a natural born athlete, just like your father," Zach's grandfather said proudly. "I never saw such talent and energy!"

"You pitched this game with better concentration," his father added as they drove past Sunset House. "You sure Pete won't join us for lunch?"

"He's too exhausted. I'll bike over after the cookout. He won't believe we beat the Tigers by one run."

"Picking Pete must be well into his eighties by now. I heard him perform when your grandmother and I were still in college."

130

"Speaking of old people, Dad, I've got a special present for your birthday."

"Keeping your cool and winning that ball game is the best present I can think of, Zipper!"

Zach grinned. This was going to be a great day. He stared out the van window and thought about his father's birthday party. He imagined sitting on the swing set with Josh eating juicy hot dogs and humungous slices of chocolate cake. Zach imagined climbing on his drum stool, plant light focused on his face, playing the birthday rap on high hat and snare drums. He imagined his mother putting her soft arms around his neck and whispering that he'd made the whole family proud.

21.

Monday night Zach sat on his bed surrounded by stacks of baseball cards. He slipped a new rookie card into his daily planner to show to Josh. Pulling his science report on electricity from his backpack, he thumbed through the pages. He'd gotten an A+. Mrs. Ginsberg had asked Zach to read the report in front of the entire class.

Zach was so focused on his baseball cards, he didn't hear his mother's voice. "Telephone for Zipper," she yelled again up the stairs.

"Thanks for inviting me to your cookout," Josh said. "I really liked your grandfather."

Zach paced around his parents' double bed, twisting the phone cord. "Wasn't it funny when Gramps played my drums? He loves jazz. Someday he might *buy* me a drum set! He thinks I'm real talented."

"Isabel says your drums are making her deaf."

"She's such a wimp! She just wants to get me in trouble. She didn't have to tell Mom it was my finger-prints on the pink icing."

"I think your dad liked his birthday rap," Josh said.

"Liked it. He loved it! I'm getting into body language. I know what people are thinking just by watching them."

"Want to come for a sleep-over Saturday after the game?" Josh asked.

"Sure, I'll come."

"My brother, Simon, is inviting his friend Buck to sleep over too. He's the fat guy we went fishing with."

"You mean that creep who stole all my worms? I hate that kid."

"He's okay once you get to know him."

Zach lay on his back with his feet up on the wall, trying to untwist the telephone cord. "I've got a sur-prise to show you. I'll bring it to homework club to-morrow," he said, hanging up the phone.

Skipping back into his bedroom, Zach turned up the volume on the radio rap station. He'd never been invited to a sleep-over before, except by his cousins. Zach tapped his pencil and opened his daily planner. He'd finished all his assignments in homework club. The biography for English written in red ink wasn't due for two weeks. Zach put on his pajamas and climbed under his checkered bedspread.

The radio was blasting so loud that Zach didn't hear the knocking on his bedroom door. His father opened the door a crack. "Can we come in?" he hollered.

Zach turned down the music. His mother took off her shoes and sat down on his bed. She was holding a stack of papers. "We had a meeting with the neurologist today," she said.

"What did he say?" Zach watched his dad pace back and forth. That body language meant he was nervous.

"Dr. Murray says you definitely have that Attention Deficit Hyperactivity Disorder," his father said. He sat down in Zach's desk chair, stood up, and walked over to the window. "He says you are a very creative, intelligent boy."

"I know that, Dad. What about this disorder? What does it do to you?"

His mother pulled some papers out of a folder. "This brochure from a group called CH.A.D.D. lists the major symptoms," she said, putting on her glasses. "It says ADHD affects 3 to 5 percent of all school-age children. The major symptoms of ADHD are distractibility, impulsivity, hyperactivity, disorganization, social problems, mood swings, and difficulty with delayed gratification."

Zach sat up in bed. "What's impulsivity and all this stuff about gratification?" he asked.

His dad sensed his concern. "Not to worry! Impulsivity just means you act before you think. *Everyone* is impulsive now and then."

"You are *much* more impulsive than most kids your age, however," his mother added.

"So now what?" Zach asked.

"We have several options." His mom took a deep breath and tucked her hair behind her ears. "Dr. Murray says some kids respond wonderfully to medication. Other kids learn to become more self-controlled and better focused without taking any pills."

"I know a kid at school who takes a brain pill every day at lunch time. He says it helps him concentrate."

"He may be taking Ritalin. Dr. Murray says it works miracles for certain children."

"Can I take Ritalin?" Zach asked. "I'd take a pill five times a day if it kept me out of trouble."

"Ritalin does have certain side effects, like loss of appetite and difficulty getting to sleep at night."

"I've got a great appetite," Zach said, "but I already have problems getting to sleep."

"We haven't made any decisions," his father interrupted. "First we need to talk again to Mrs. Ginsberg

135

and the people at school. We have another meeting with the neurologist next week."

"Can I come? Don't you think I should be part of making this decision?"

"Absolutely," his father agreed. "The more I read about ADHD, the more I suspect that I have it as well. That's why I became a builder. No way could I stay cooped up in an office all day."

"By the way," his mother said, "Dr. Murray considers playing the drums an excellent way to channel your physical energies." She glanced at her husband. "But don't YOU get any ideas about renting a set!"

"Is this your science project?" His dad picked up a folder from the desk, the one with the zigzag lightning bolt on the cover. "Mrs. Ginsberg tells us that you wrote an excellent report."

"And you passed it in on time!" his mother said proudly. "Incidentally, Mrs. Ginsberg says you don't have to go to homework club anymore. She told us that ever since you started really using that daily planner, almost every assignment has been passed in on time."

"Suppose I *want* to go to homework club?"

"I'm sure they won't kick you out!" his dad replied.

After his parents had left the room, Zach lay on his side and listened for the cicada bugs. Once you could hear their shrill chirp, it meant summer vacation was about to begin. He wondered what kids would think if he started taking Ritalin pills at Boy Scout camp. It made him feel good to know that what he felt inside his head had a name. He wasn't alone. It wasn't all his fault. Other kids had thoughts banging around like hockey pucks in their brains too.

22.

Zach felt his mother's hand gently rubbing his back. "Time to get up," she whispered. Zach sat up in bed and rubbed his eyes. He had slept in his Boy Scout uniform so that he wouldn't forget to wear it to school.

"I've got some good news. Last night at the Fourth of July Float Committee meeting, we voted unanimously to ask Picking Pete to ride on the Valley School float. Students from the school orchestra and the Recorder Club will be invited to accompany him."

"What about me? Aren't I going to play my drums?"

"I imagine if Pete wants drum backup, you'd be the logical choice. After all, you've been practicing to his music day and night."

Zach jumped out of bed and pulled his daily planner out of his backpack. "After Boy Scouts, I'll write down to visit Sunset House. I'll tell Pete the good news."

"I think the committee chairperson has written him a letter."

"I'll have to read the letter to Pete. He's a smart man but he dropped out of school to earn money. His daughter is the first person in the family to go to college. Besides, now Pete's so old his eyes went bad." Zach sat on the side of the bed and tied his sneakers.

"Don't forget to go to Scouts." His mother picked up a wicker laundry basket. "Your dad's cooking supper tonight. I won't get home until late. Don't forget to brush your teeth. Be a good boy in school."

Zach wished his mother would quit reminding him to be good. Did she think he messed up on purpose, like it was fun to go to the principal's office? Zach combed the hair out of his eyes and fed Moby a pinch of fish food. After eating a bowl of Cheerios, he spread peanut butter between two slices of bread.

"The bus is here," Isabel called.

Grabbing his jacket and backpack, Zach rushed out the front door. In the school bus, he noticed that Charlie had gotten another haircut. He was about to point and giggle, but he stopped himself. He took a deep breath and walked by without saying a word. Frankie, Leroy, and Guy were waiting for Zach at the back of the bus. They had begun to sit with Zach in the last row so they could talk about baseball without being overheard by girls.

After Scouts, Zach walked downtown to Sunset House. He stopped to pull weeds from the flower bed, then noticed that Pete's rocking chair was empty. "Where's Pete?" he called to Daisy. Daisy rocked back and forth. She hardly seemed to hear. "Where is Pete?" Zach repeated in a louder voice. Daisy put her knitting in her lap.

"Pete's gone," she whispered in a frail voice. Wisps of yellow hair fell across her lined face.

"Gone? You mean he went inside to the bathroom?"

Daisy shook her head. "Flashing lights. Flashing lights took Pete away."

Zach leapt up the porch steps. He ran to Mrs. Brendle's office and pounded on the door.

"Where did they take Pete?" he cried.

Mrs. Brendle opened the office door. "Zipper, I'm so glad you came. I wasn't sure how to get in touch with you."

"What happened?" Zach's heart pounded. "Is Pete okay?"

Mrs. Brendle ran her tongue over her lips. She spoke in a slow, steady voice. "It looks serious, Zipper.

Last night Pete had a massive heart attack. His daughter just called to report that he is in critical condition."

Zach slumped into a chair. "He said he didn't feel well. I just thought he had an upset stomach or a headache, something like that, nothing serious."

"Pete must have had an idea that something was wrong. He wrote you this note yesterday." Mrs. Brendle took a letter off her desk and handed it to Zach. The word "Zipy" was written on the outside of the envelope in crooked handwriting.

Zipy,
    If somthin shud happin, Bandit
is yours.
                    Love,
                    Pete

Zach read the note twice. "Thanks Mrs. Brendle," he said. "Can I go into Pete's room? He wants me to take something home."

"I hope it's that bird."

"You know about Bandit?" Zach asked in a surprised voice.

"Oh, I've known about that bird all along. It gave Pete such pleasure." Mrs. Brendle smiled. "Pete is such a dear man. Did you know that Daisy taught him to knit? Before his eyes got so bad, he knit his daughter a lovely purple scarf. Everyone here loves him."

"Pete is one of the few grownups who believes in me." Zach looked down at the rug and shuffled his feet. "He says I've got rhythm like Baby Dodds. He says my bones are stuffed with talent. I got my drum set because of Picking Pete."

"He loves your visits. We all do, Zipper. Promise me that you'll keep dropping by even while Pete is in the hospital?"

"Pete would want me to keep an eye on Daisy. I'll practice my drums and write a special rap tune just for Pete. We'll have a surprise party when he gets back from the hospital! All the Sunset residents and my parents and my little sister can come. I'll perform on the front porch. We'll get balloons and serve refreshments."

"We can even invite Bandit!" Mrs. Brendle put her arm around Zach's shoulder and walked beside him toward Pete's bedroom. The bed was unmade and papers were scattered on the floor. Pete's red suspenders were draped over his leather chair. Zach found Bandit's cage hanging in the bathroom. He said good-bye to Mrs. Brendle and carried the bird down the long, dark corridor to the front door.

Daisy looked up from her knitting. "Where are you taking that bird?" she asked crossly.

"Pete wants me to take care of Bandit until he gets out of the hospital."

Daisy looked back at her knitting. "Bring that bird back tomorrow," she said. "Pete's coming back tomorrow."

When Zach got home, he found a note taped to the back door. His dad had left to drive Liz home for supper. He carried the birdcage up to his bedroom. Zach wondered if Pete would be well enough to ride on the Fourth of July float. He started to make a get well card but his mind wandered. Instead, Zach filled up every square inch of space on his desk blotter with doodles.

23.

Isabel walked into her brother's bedroom. "How do you spell ridiculous?" she asked. "I'm writing about a ridiculous rat in my bonus spelling sentences and. . . ." Isabel froze. She stared at the cage. "Where did you get that bird?" she cried.

"Picking Pete wants me to take care of it. He went to the hospital. He's got a heart attack but he's going to be just fine."

"Mom told me about your disease," Isabel said in a low voice. "I'm sorry I teased you. Mom said that when you act weird, it's not always your fault."

Zach wiggled his foot. "ADHD isn't a disease!" he protested. He paused and then added, "Mom is right. You shouldn't tease me so much."

"So when will you be able to sit still and act normal?"

Unsure whether Isabel was being thoughtful or really mean, Zach didn't know how to reply. He picked up his pencil and continued to doodle on his desk blotter.

"I'd still rather have a dog than a brother," Isabel muttered as she walked back into her room.

Zach unlatched the birdcage door and let Bandit fly free. Disoriented and confused, she flitted frantically from the bookcase to his desk to the window. She flew toward the light and banged into the window pane. Afraid she might get hurt, Zach tried to lure Bandit back into the cage. Quick as a fly, she darted into the closet and perched on the deck of a model aircraft carrier wedged on the top shelf. Zach slammed the closet door, trapping her inside.

Zach sat down at his desk and opened his daily planner. Making a list always helped to organize his racing thoughts.

1. get p. butter, brd seed and fres. water
2. fres. newspap. for bottom of cage
3. get lib. bk on brd care
4. wrt. card for Pete
5. ride bk to hosp.

Worried that the bird might suffocate in the closet, Zach hurried down the stairs to get his butterfly net. He remembered leaning it against snow shovels when he made the drum room. If Bandit was still free when his mother got home, there would be trouble.

"Mom hates birds," Isabel called from her room. "Remember when that sea gull pooped on her hair up in Maine?"

"Shut up!" Zach yelled as he leapt back up the stairs, two at a time.

"I'm telling Mom you said shut up."

"Isabel, this is serious. Bandit just flew into my closet and she won't come out."

"I'll get her! The man at the zoo wrapped snakes around my neck on the field trip. My teacher says I have a way with animals."

"Get the broom," Zach yelled. "We'll brush Bandit into the net."

Isabel got the broom from the cleaning closet and followed her brother back up the stairs. "This stupid net won't work!" Zach yelled. "It's got a hole." He threw the butterfly net against the closet door.

"Don't panic!" Isabel left the room and returned with a wool winter hat. She stretched it around the rim of the net and taped it on tight with masking tape. "Here," she said, "try this."

Zach held the broom in one hand and the butterfly net in the other. He cracked open the closet door. Bandit was no longer perched on the aircraft carrier. "Where is she?" he asked, peering into the closet.

"I bet she's dead!"

"Maybe she got stuck between the hangers." Zach wiggled the hangers along the pole. "Keep quiet," he whispered. "Listen for her peep." There was silence, total silence.

"You killed her!" Isabel groaned. "Even if it isn't your fault, you mess up everything. She's dead. I know it. Her little body is curled up in a giant dust ball. I'm getting Dad."

"Stay calm," Zach said. "I'll handle this." He crawled into the closet on his hands and knees. Three violent sneezes scared Bandit out of a red bedroom slipper. She flew up into Zach's face. He grabbed at her with both hands. "Open the cage!" he cried.

Isabel opened the cage as Zach thrust the bird inside. He quickly locked the latch. "Nothing to it!" he said, checking his fingers for blood.

Isabel studied the bird. "I don't think Bandit likes it here," she said.

Zach put the cage on his desk. "Sure she does! I'm calling Josh. He wants a bird too but his brother is

147

allergic to feathers. All he gets is three dumb mice. Josh can make a sketch of Bandit for Pete. He's a really good artist."

"Bandit hates it here. I know. I communicate with animals."

Zach stuck out his tongue and wiggled it in his sister's face.

"You're gross!" she cried, marching back to her room.

Zach walked into his parents' bedroom to call Josh. The red message light was blinking on the answering machine. Thinking that Coach Ward might have left a message about the baseball awards dinner, Zach pressed the play button.

"This is a message for Zipper Winson." Zach recognized Mrs. Brendle's voice even though it sounded like she had a cold. "Pete's daughter has informed us that her father passed away at 4:37 this afternoon. He died peacefully. I wanted Zipper to know." The red light stopped blinking and the answering machine clicked off.

Zach caught his breath. The news hit him like a punch in the stomach. His heart pounded and his hands got sticky with sweat. He thought he should cry. He blinked but his eyes stayed perfectly dry.

Zach walked on jello legs to the cellar. He picked
up his drum sticks and slowly pounded out a string of
double paradiddles. Then he turned on Picking Pete's
records, one after another, and pounded his drums to
the tune of the slide guitar. When he played the drums,

he felt set free from the ideas other people had of him. Pete said he'd go places, as long as he put his mind to it. He vowed never to let Pete down. He'd get real drum lessons, pitch for the All Stars, and make more friends, even run for student council. He'd prove to Pete and to the world that a kid with ADHD could make it big.

Upstairs in his bedroom, Zach hoisted the screen on his window. He carried the bird cage to the window sill. "You should be free," he said to Bandit. "You should take control of your life just like I'm taking control of mine." With those words, he opened the cage door. As Bandit flew free, Zach's eyes filled up with tears.

Appendix

You might want to read this part of my book with your Mom or Dad or another grown-up. I'll answer questions that my students and my sons have asked me about ways to understand and cope with problems paying attention.

What is ADHD?

Everyone has different learning strengths and weaknesses. People with Attention Deficit Hyperactivity Disorder (ADHD) tend to have average to above average intelligence. Even though children with ADHD are intelligent, they sometimes have difficulty making friends and staying focused in school. Their attention hops from place to place and idea to idea. In many cases, ADHD runs in the family. That means you can inherit ADHD. Experts think that ADHD is caused by a biochemical difference in the brain. It affects from 3 to 5 percent of school-aged kids, most of them boys. The major symptoms of ADHD are inappropriate inattention, impulsivity, and hyperactivity. What exactly do these words mean? Turn the page to find out!

Inattention

People with ADHD have difficulty "tuning out" unimportant sights, smells, and sounds coming into the brain. They have trouble focusing on one thing at a time, even when it is important to pay attention. That's why Zipper got distracted by chirping birds instead of listening to his teacher. Problems with paying attention may range from mild to quite severe. It is usually easier to concentrate or re-focus yourself on tasks you enjoy. For example, Zipper was super-focused while playing Nintendo and his drums. Doctors consider the possibility that ADHD might be present if six or more of the following symptoms of inattention have lasted for longer than six months...

- ✯ often fails to pay close attention to details and makes careless mistakes;
- ✯ often has difficulty sustaining attention to tasks;
- ✯ often does not seem to listen even when spoken to directly;
- ✯ often does not follow through on instructions and has trouble finishing school work and chores (not because you don't want to!);
- ✯ often has difficulty organizing tasks and activities;

⭐ often avoids or dislikes tasks that require sustained effort (like schoolwork and homework);

⭐ often loses things necessary for a task—like books and pencils;

⭐ is often distracted by sights and sounds around them;

⭐ is often forgetful in daily activities.

Impulsivity & Hyperactivity

I'm sure you also noticed that Zipper was impulsive and hyperactive. He acted impulsively when he did or said things without thinking about the consequences. For example, he said that Wilma's face was "as wrinkled as a dried prune." He never stopped to think how a comment like that might make Wilma feel. Zipper was also hyperactive. He would pace, wiggle, fidget, and squirm all day long. It's like his brain's accelerator system was stuck on "full steam ahead." That's why kids with ADHD have so much trouble "putting on the brakes." Doctors consider the possibility that ADHD might be present if six or more of the following symptoms of impulsivity and hyperactivity have lasted longer than six months...

impulsivity

- ✦ often blurts out answers before questions have been completed;
- ✦ often has difficulty waiting his or her turn;
- ✦ often interrupts or intrudes (i.e., butts into conversations or games).

hyperactivity

- ✦ often fidgets with hands or feet or squirms in seat;
- ✦ often gets up when he or she is supposed to stay seated;
- ✦ often runs around or climbs on things when it is not appropriate;
- ✦ often has difficulty playing quietly;
- ✦ often acts "on the go" as if "driven by a motor;"
- ✦ often talks too much.

Are There Different Types of ADHD?

Yes! There are three different types of ADHD. Some kids have difficulty paying attention but no problem with hyperactivity and impulsivity. Other children have hyperactivity and impulsivity but no problem paying attention. A third group of children have hyperactivity, impulsivity, and problems paying attention. Sometimes the term Attention Deficit Disorder (ADD) is used to describe these types of problems.

How Do I Know If I Have ADD or ADHD?

If you have had behavioral and attentional problems at home and at school, it is important to talk to an expert like a neurologist, pediatrician, psychologist, or counselor. Sometimes it is difficult to make a diagnosis in the doctor's office because kids with ADHD are often very intelligent and appropriate while working one-on-one with an adult. The doctor will rely on a detailed list of symptoms from your parents and teachers. Information from a team of specialists is helpful in diagnosing learning and attentional problems. This information may include a physical exam and tests of your hearing and vision. You may also take tests to measure your intellectual potential and how well you are doing in your school work. One important clue is to see if your problems with attention and behavior started before the age of 7 and if they have lasted for at least 6 months. Some kids become worried or sad because of upsetting events in their life such as a move, a death, or a divorce. They, too, can show symptoms of inattention, impulsivity, and hyperactivity. That is why ADHD can be tricky to recognize and diagnose.

What Is the Best Treatment for ADHD?

Many experts believe the best treatment for ADHD is to combine ways to change your behavior with the use of medication. Kids can learn strategies to improve their focus, impulse control, and organization. Think of what is hard for you and then brainstorm with your parents and teachers possible ways to make the situation better. You may find the following suggestions helpful...

Ideas to Improve Your School Success

- ✦ Decide how you study best; some kids like total silence while other kids think better with background music.
- ✦ Break long assignments into small chunks; don't wait until the last minute to study for a test.
- ✦ When you study, take timed "activity breaks"; figure out a good homework routine and stick with it.

✸ Ask your teachers for help; there are special ways to instruct and reward students who don't like repetition and need to move around.

✸ Don't sit next to people or things that distract you; keep the top of your desk clear and the inside organized, not a "black hole!"

✸ Write down all homework; the daily planner helped Zipper remember his baseball glove as well as his math assignments.

✸ Learn computer skills; proofread for mistakes; use spellcheck!

Ideas to Improve Your Social Success

✸ Pay attention to the rules and what kind of behavior is expected (i.e., playground vs. classroom).

✸ Read non-verbal "body language" like facial expressions, tone of voice; respect the "personal space" of your friends.

✸ Be a good listener even when people disagree with you.

✸ If you get really mad, hold your breath and count to 10 before you do or say anything... think of the consequences! (Will your response get you in trouble or make you feel proud?)

✯ Learn ways to calm down when you get frustrated or angry (i.e., punch a pillow, run around the block, listen to music, breathe deeply, draw a picture, write a poem, talk to your dog or someone you trust).

✯ Be a good sport and say congratulations, even when you lose.

✯ Practice being a mind reader—try to figure out what other people are feeling; say a kind word to a kid who needs a friend.

✯ Learn to name your feelings; don't be afraid to ask for help if you fell angry or sad or misunderstood.

Medication

For children with ADHD, a group of medications known as stimulants such as Ritalin, Dexedrine, Cylert, and Adderall can be helpful. Other medications such as anti-depressants and blood pressure medicines have also been found to help people with ADHD. These medications help the body become less restless and the mind more alert and attentive. Some children may experience side effects from taking medication. Common side effects are loss of appetite, stomach aches, head aches, and for some medications, difficulty falling asleep. If you experience these or other side effects, it is important to tell your parents and to inform your doctor. The doctor may change the dosage of the medication or prescribe a different medication if the side effects really bother you. Some kids feel comfortable about taking medications while other kids feel awkward and worried. It is important to talk to a grown-up about your feelings. Medication is said to reduce the symptoms of ADHD at least 70 percent of the time. Medication has the power to improve your body's ability to slow down and pay attention.

A Tribute to Jamie

Our son Jamie was diagnosed with ADHD when he was in the first grade. I wrote this book in honor of the wonderful way that Jamie has taken control of his life. Like other people with ADHD, his brain has pockets of amazing creativity, energy, insightfulness, and determination. Once Jamie learned to understand what was going on inside his head, he figured out ways to cope with his attentional problems. As you may have guessed, Jamie had a passion for playing the drums! He now plays 38 percussive instruments including the hammered dulcimer, didjeridoo, tablas, congas, and bongos. After graduating from college, Jamie moved to Boulder, Colorado, where he built a career he loves, performing and selling his music. He sits in with the band called PHISH and has formed Realm Records, sold world-wide by a big record company. With his hard work, free spirit, and abounding energy, Jamie has made his whole family so proud!

Resources

Organizations

ADDA (Attention Deficit Disorder Association)
P.O. Box 972
Mentor, OH 44061
800-487-2282

CHADD (Children and Adults with Attention Deficit
Disorder)
499 NW 70th Avenue, Suite 308
Plantation, FL 33317
305-587-3700

LDA (Learning Disabilities Association)
4156 Library Road
Pittsburgh, PA 15234
412-341-1515

ADD Warehouse
300 NW 70th Avenue, Suite 102
Plantation, FL 33317
800-233-9273
This is an excellent source for books and videos on
the topic of ADD/ADHD.

Suggested Reading for Parents and Teachers

Bain, L., *A Parent's Guide to Attention Deficit Disorder*, Bantam Doubleday Dell Publishing Group, Inc., 1991.

Barkley, R., *Taking Charge of ADHD: The Complete, Authoritative Guide for Parents*, Guilford Press, 1995.

Garber, S., et. al, *Beyond Ritalin: Facts about Medication and Other Strategies for Helping Children, Adolescents, and Adults with Attention Deficit Disorder*, Harper Collins, 1997.

Hallowell, E. and Ratey, T., *Driven to Distraction: Recognizing and Coping with Attention Deficit Disorder from Childhood through Adulthood*, Touchstone, 1994.

Parker, H., *The ADD Hyperactivity Handbook for Schools*, Specialty Press, 1992.

Rief, S., *How to Reach and Teach ADD/ADHD Children*, The Center for Applied Research in Education, 1993.

Silver, L., *Dr. Larry Silver's Advice to Parents on Attention Deficit Hyperactivity Disorder,* American Psychiatric Press, Inc., 1993.

Taylor, J., *Helping Your Hyperactive/Attention Deficit Child,* Second Edition, Prima, 1997.

Vail, P., *Smart Kids with School Problems,* E.P. Dutton, 1987.

Winebrenner, S., *Teaching Kids with Learning Difficulties in the Regular Classroom,* Free Spirit Publishing, 1996.

Suggested Reading for Kids

Caffrey, J., *First Star I See,* Verbal Images Press, 1997.

Cummings, R., and Fisher, G., *The School Survival Guide for Kids with LD (Learning Differences),* Free Spirit Publishing, 1991.

Gehret, J., *Eagle Eyes: A Child's Guide to Paying Attention,* Verbal Images Press, 1996.

Levine, M., *Keeping Ahead in School: A Student's Book about Learning Abilities and Learning Disorders,* Educators Publishing Services, Inc., 1990.

Nadeau, K., and Dixon, E., *Learning to Slow Down and Pay Attention: A Book for Kids about ADD,* Second Edition, Magination Press, 1997.

Parker, H., *The ADD Hyperactivity Workbook for Parents, Teachers, and Kids,* Impact Publications, 1988.

Quinn, P., and Stern, J., *Putting on the Brakes: Young People's Guide to Understanding Attention Deficit Hyperactivity Disorder,* Magination Press, 1991.

About the Author

Caroline Janover grew up with a learning difference in a small town in New Hampshire. Her second year in the second grade, she invented her own private language and began to write nightly in locked diaries. As the mother of two bright, creative, dyslexic sons, Caroline now weaves real-life experiences into fiction as she writes about the triumphs of young people who struggle to pay attention and to learn in school. Caroline is also the author of *The Worst Speller in Jr. High* (Free Spirit Publishing, 1995) and *Josh, A Boy with Dyslexia* (Waterfront Books, 1988).

A graduate of Sarah Lawrence College, Caroline received Master's Degrees from Boston University and Fairleigh Dickinson University. She currently lives with her husband in Ridgewood, NJ where she is a Learning Disabilities Teacher/ Consultant in the public school system. A recipient of the Governor's Outstanding Teacher Award, Caroline lectures nationally to children, parents, and teachers about the perceptual problems and creative strengths of children with ADHD and dyslexia.